ONE WELCOME CHILD:
A Love Story

By

James Louis Fortuna, Jr.

Lightnin' Bug Publishing
Statesville, North Carolina

Lightnin' Bug Publishing
Statesville, North Carolina

This is a work of fiction. Any similarity of name or action described herein to any person, living or dead, is entirely coincidental.

Address all correspondence c/o Lightin' Bug Publishing, lightninbug@att.net.

First Lightnin' Bug Edition: 2023
ISBN: 9798374706925

This novel is dedicated to men and women who recognize the unitive/procreative purpose of marriage–and to those brave souls who pray outside abortion clinics.

Author's Preface

One Welcome Child is set in a fictional Southeast Georgia. The Theme is an ancient but common one best phrased by a question: Without God—who ultimately gives value to human life?

James Louis Fortuna, Jr.
Winston-Salem, North Carolina
2022

PROLOGUE

Freedom Highway

The runaways had hidden in the woods behind the Condom City parking lot, just past the line of dumpsters but not so far into the pine and scrub to keep the truck lights from finding the sparkle their pajamas made. Parker Sledge had seen them first and leaned his head out on the driver's side to whistle like a whippoorwill and tongue a cluck-cluck chicken sound that brought back giggles when he quit. Emment Colvard shook his head and sighed.

"You want me to gather 'em in, Mr. Sledge?"

"No—not quite yet. They're close on ready though. Hear that?"

The giggles had begun to drop off into humming, bee-hive steady in the little breeze that came up strong enough to make the lower pine boughs dance and jump. It was getting colder by the second, Parker's skin a tingle on the metal of the door, his fingers cold and drumming to the rhythm that the runaways set down. Emment sounded tired as always of the way it had to be. But the two out yonder in the pines would need some extra care, first-timers, numbers nine and ten so far this month. Not one had made it further than the Rainbow Strip.

"Why'n ya just let me go on an' get 'em, Mr. Sledge? I can do it quick."

"No—no they need to hum awhile. They don't like the dark. That's why they ended up out here. Every time. The lights—"

It was well past two o'clock, past closing-time for almost all the places on the Strip, the Condom City lot near empty and the porn shops and the abortion and STD clinics closing one by one, their lights a broken smear of blurry color right and left behind the truck. The humming wavered, stop and start and giggles breaking in again this time to answer Parker's hoot-owl cries. He had been asleep and dreaming of the eagles out on Sutter's Swamp, the one or two still left back in the cypress that Medix couldn't touch. Big Nurse's voice had brought him up just when the smallest eagle noticed he was there.

"Mr. Sledge—oh Mr. Sledge!"

"Huh—wha? I'm—I'm coming—"

And she had waved her arms and choked the words out in a coughing gasp, her face one tremble-roll of fat and twitching down her puffy cheeks and on her chin and bobbing on her housecoat collar front to back. The runaways had made their break while she was with the babies in the Bull Rush Ward.

"I—I—I—didn't notice—not—not un-til—until a few—just now—just when I went to—back to make my rounds—"

These two had never tried a break before, a full year and a few weeks more or less, both well-behaved and never any trouble to the staff. But once they started in to run or hop or crawl away it seemed they never were the same again. And this year more had tried it than in all the fifteen years together in a lump, single and in twos, fours and twice in sixes from the Big Boys' Honor Barn. He knew the lights had done it to them all, the Strip that stretched out closer every day it seemed, a flashing on the sky toward Carver City down along the Freedom Highway with a tug and pull inside it strong enough to touch first one and then another of the children with an almost lust to go and see. And it was getting worse and worse.

"Can y'see 'em still, Mr. Sledge?"

"Oh yes—yes. They're standing up now.'

"It kills me how they do that—I mean I've seen it an' don't hardly believe it. Only two legs between 'em—one on each—a left an' a right—two lefts or two rights even. I've seen that a few times—at play-period. Hoppin' like two-headed kangaroos. God. It's crazy—"

"It's the lights that make them run away."

Condom City had opened first of all the rest, the new Georgia state law and changes in the county zoning and the land next door sold quick and on the quiet by the heirs of old Judge Finch, all going in together with the clinics needing room to grow. The porn shops had been next to come and bars not far behind, the Triple-X Motel the latest with its steel and concrete tower rising from the fringes of the swamp and pushing out into a short and wing-like bulge of shopping mall that advertised divorce in just one day and all the newest lingerie. And lights and more lights everywhere for both north and south and billboards flashing out the mileage for the soldier boys and sailors further down the coast. It had nearly reached the gates of Kiddie Kuntry, just one last stretch of pine and scrub-oak there, palmetto dotted and the Georgia red clay free of asphalt where his own land rimmed the Condom City lot and curved back in a narrow sweep to what was left of Sutter's Swamp. Of southeast Georgia like it used to look.

"Want me to get 'em now?"

"Just a minute more. They're almost ready. You can hear that yourself. They're tired and frightened."

"Yes sir. Phew—goin' full blast tonight back yonder by th'smell of it."

"Yes. Full again. It's Sunday. Burning day. We'll check the bins before we go. But look—there—they're coming out—see? No—I'll go get them. When they clear the trees."

He glanced in the rear-view mirror just in time to see a burst of flame die quickly, black smoke thick and steady in behind, a boiling in the bright lights near the biggest clinic there. The smoke would puff for hours, the stench all thick and riding on the breeze. And then the stench would go away, by dawn the fires would start to cool, a fine ash left to sweep or wash down to the gutters when the Strip began its day. The runaways were almost at the dumpsters now.

"Lookit 'em go—God, Mr. Sledge—they don't look bigger'n rabbits."

"That's Gemma-Girl with the right leg—and the other one—the left leg must be Jesse-Lee."

And then he stepped down from the truck, the door left open and its mirror showing just the bottom of the Condom City sign, reversed in slowly flashing colors, a giant penis sheaved in red and blue and green and gold. The runaways were in a chirping sound ahead, a tap and tap of bare feet on the hard-packed clay out where the dumpsters stood, the light a shimmer in the smoky air like ghosts at play upon the wind. And Mr.

Parker Sledge knelt down and waited for his babies to come home.

PART ONE

The Parker Sledge Story

CHAPTER ONE

She had tried to kiss his hand, escaping Big Nurse at the doorway of the guest-house in an almost blur of hair and feathers, a scent of cinnamon about her then in reaching out and making just a little cry the way the children did when they got scared. But Big Nurse came down quick behind and helped her on inside. The guest-house had been shut up tight for months and smelled of mold. But a fire was crackling in the woodstove near the door and the girl had smiled and waved when Parker had finally left, Big Nurse there beside her humming softly, moving her gently toward the bed. The door had shut too quickly, a gust of wind come up to make it groan and creak and slam to with a flat sound, loud and touched by echoes in the darkness of the porch. And Parker had left to check the runaways again, the babies right-leg/left-leg, Gemma-Girl and Jesse-Lee still sleeping deep two corridors apart and Emment steady on the watch between. The girl had come when they got back, not right at first but later on, Parker finally in his room, a knocking loud then soft that brought him up from staring at the curling flames inside the fireplace Emment built the year the Strip began to grow. Parker had never seen a girl with eyes that big before.

"Can—can you help me? Please, mister—please?"

Her voice had seemed older than the way she looked, a husky sound that didn't fit the feathered dress or green and glittered cape-like shawl that covered up her long black hair that hung in tassels down her arms. The feathers had splayed in the wind, pulling right and left and up and down, the dress a silver one, thin and ripped along the sides. Her face was long, skin dark, cheeks roughed red, nose a strong one, slightly arched but ending in a pinkish ball that dipped each time she spoke. He hadn't heard a car and every gate was locked.

"How—how did you get here?"

"Through the fence—back there—a hole—a little hole—near too little. Look—I need help—please—let me in Ok? Just to get warm? Ok?"

Her smile had surprised him, wide and showing many teeth then gone as quick as it had come. Parker had pushed the button on the wall, the first one in the box that signaled Big Nurse or whoever else might be there watching in the Bull Rush Ward. And then he had let the girl come in and stirred the fire until it popped and hissed. As he had turned around and sat down on the fireplace ledge he noticed that her legs were muddy, knees all scratched and caked in dirt and clay.

"You can sit there." He had motioned to a high-backed chair below the signal box. "I've called for one of the staff. They'll be along directly. You say you got in through a hole?"

"Yeah—a—a little one." She had pulled the shawl-cape tighter on her shoulders and then shuffled to the chair, shoes a purple color flecked with orange stars. "Down yonder from the road and them big pines—I fell—an' there it was—"

"You been in an accident?"

"Pardon me?" She had sat very still, knees together and the dress and feathers mixed up in a whirl of different colors, shoes in painful clash with all the rest. He noticed that she wasn't wearing any rings at all, no jewelry on her hands or ears or neck.

"Accident—did you wreck your car?" Something about her had seemed familiar, there for just a second and then gone among a pop and crackle from the fire. "Flat tire maybe? Engine trouble? We don't get too many walk-ins here."

Just two in all the time since Kiddie Kuntry opened up for real, with license from the county and the state and two fat grants that helped him build the things he needed for the babies sure to come. But only two of them had ever walked in on their own. In all that time just two. The first a one-eyed black boy with a head stuck on all wrong, an angle to his neck that made his good eye seem forever focused on the ground. The second had been mostly white and younger, armless but for flippers dangling from his shoulders like two mittens covered up in fur. This girl was older than the both of them and everything seemed in its proper place; but at the first he felt that she belonged, a something in the smile and wide, wide eyes had made him want to keep her there, just like the other two and just as long.

"I—I ain't got no place 'round here I can hide—an' I ain't had no time to think. Y'see, I only just found out for sure tonight. Copper found out too—I don't know how he did it so quick but he did—so—so I run off—"

"Is he your boyfriend?"

"What?"

"Copper. Is he your boyfriend?"

"Copper? Lor' God no—no—my God! Copper my boyfriend? No!" Her laugh had come in like a ripple in the words, before and in between and nearly like the giggle-sound the runaways had made. The fire had broken in the middle then, a fat oak log cut clean in two, its smoking ends down in among the coals with tips that splayed out sparkles in the dark above. He had dropped a shorter log between them and turned back to watch the girl. "Copper my boyfriend—whew!" She had lowered the shawl-cape, hair all thick and shiny black and curling down into the feathers bunched up on her chest. She had shifted position when she brushed her fingers through her hair, a brief, the very briefest show of red back deep between her legs, then feathers and the silver cloth pulled down and smoothed out to her knees together once again. "He's my bossman at the Silver Beaver—I'm a dancer there. He's got all th'specialty acts."

"You're a dancer?"

"Hey don't sound so surprised—I don't always look like this." She had brushed a few times at her lap, shawl-cape slipping down a short way on her arms.

"I—I'm sorry—I didn't mean to—" He had squirmed a bit and moved further from the fire. His face felt hot and he had tried to say some more but she cut him off before the first word made it out.

"That's Ok—I'm only teasing." The smile had stayed longer than before, her tongue flicked out a few times toward the end in quick sweeps on her lips from side to side. "I got the midnight run over there—lucky to get it too. I mostly do the ac/dc crowd—except tonight." She had folded the shawl-cape on her lap, long fingers pressed together there on top. "Tonight I came in too late—tried to sneak in but he caught me. An' he a'ready knew where I'd been. I don't know how—maybe one of the waitresses—they're all th'time lookin' to be dancers, y'know. Maybe that red-headed bitch he just put to workin' the Be-Bop Lounge. She's all th'time watchin' me dance."

"So—Copper's your boss?"

"Yeah—un-til tonight. He said I'd just have to get fixed permanent—y'know—clean-out time and so forth? Y'see I'm further along this go round—it don't show but I am. Th'nurse told me—finally—you gotta wait forever at Medix—made me later'n hell too an' then Copper a'ready knew anyways—"

"So you're—"

"Right. Knocked-up again. Second time in three years. Copper was not pleased." The laugh was close on a cough this time, a raspy-gargle and her hands had fluttered out across her lap.

"Does the father—"

"I don't know the daddy. Not for sure anyways. It might have been anybody—I—I got careless at the beach—near as I can figure out it was over there. Had me too good a time—I—look—" The tears had seemed to almost spring out from a sudden bunching of the skin across her cheeks, eyes nearly lost and rouge in narrow streaks begun to push down toward the tremble of her chin. Her words had stuck and tumbled as they came. "Can't I—I just—just stay here—for—for a few days? I—I—can sleep—any-where—right here on the floor. Just a few days—just till Copper gets tired a looking. I've—I've got a cousin in North Carolina. I think she'll take me in. For awhile. An'—an' I—I got other friends—up north. I—I got money too—I can pay—please? I—I need to stay away—th'Beaver ain't no good for me right now—I—I need to think—" She had wiped at her face with the shawl-cape and sniffled just the way that Gemma-Girl had done back in the truck, down in the blanket-nest that Emment made. The girl had smeared the rouge around with her finger-tips, dabbing at the wet still there until it went away. And then her eyes had widened as she tried to smile. "I—I'm sorry—dumpin' on you—but—but I just can't go back there—not tonight anyways."

"Will you keep the baby?"

He had meant to ask another thing, to pat her hand or hug her close and say the needful thing to keep the tears from coming back. To comfort her like he would do with any child that cried. Just like the others who had walked in from the dark. But something made him hesitate, the difference in a feeling there from long ago that came to make him leave all that undone and watch her eyes instead, grown wider even than before and eyebrows nearly lost beneath a sweep of thick black hair. And then she frowned them into slits and slowly shook her head.

"I—I don't know. Prob'ly not. Prob'ly give it up—if—if it turns out all right. If it ain't brain-damaged or somethin' else. Y'see—I—I sometimes drink too much. Like the TV says you ain't supposed to do? Now I don't smoke no more—well maybe a joint ever now an' again—if I can trust it. That ain't the same as really smokin' though. Not to my way of thinking. There ain't no tobacco in it. But I do like my vodka. You got any?" Her face had changed back like it was before, eyes wide again and nose a bob of pink and fingers clasped together on her lap.

"No—we don't—"

"I didn't think so—but y'don't never know if y'don't

ast. Right?"

"Yes."

The feeling somehow strengthened in her words, had gotten stronger in the sound she made, her fingers long and sometimes twisting on her lap outside the place the baby grew, her belly seeming larger than before as if the telling him had made it swell, had let him see the truth of what she said. The feeling had been gone a long long time. But somehow there it was again alive and growing in her words, just like her baby growing with each breath she took, the feeling reaching for him steady on and sure and passing easy through the things he'd put up one by one to keep it well outside. Gone through them all a single jump from when his wife had run away.

"What is this place anyways? A school?"

"What?" He had forced himself to look away, to focus on the box above her head. Big Nurse had seemed to take forever getting there.

"This place—is it a school?"

"Oh—no. Not like a regular school, that is. No—it's mostly a home. For children."

"No shit? Like an orphanage?"

"Not exactly—it's not exactly an orphanage either." A memory of the County Home had tried to come in strong, to push aside the feeling in a rush of old-time pain like what had been there when his parents had gone off for good. But nothing showed beyond a first sharp flash of iron bed and window-bars, then dropping off and dimming all the rest and sinking deep inside her words.

"You part of some kind of church?"

"What?"

"Church—you ain't a preacher or somethin' are you?"

"No." He had laughed and glanced down at her face for just a blinking-time and back, her eyes turned on him straight and wider than before.

"Y'see—I ast that 'cause I ain't had no luck with preachers. I never know what they want me to say. An' I ain't never got it right. Not one damned time. Y'know what I mean?"

"Yes." The preachers at the County Home had always come for Sunday dinner, sitting at the big high table in the back and eating fast like nothing might be there past one more bite and chew and swallow. But like the bed and bars no preacher-face would stay, not one was strong enough to make it up from where he wanted them to be, down low and lost within the crackle of the fire and every sound the girl had made.

"I just ain't no good at all with preachers."

She had spread the shawl-cape out about her knees, the tassels reaching almost to the floor, her face then calm and wide eyes still there boring in to stay each time he slipped down from the box. And then her words had fanned the feeling to a blaze, the years dissolved and the wife, Martha, newly gone and him set wandering through the dark, alone and needing just a touch beside him there, the pressure of a woman's hand and feel of flesh against him when he turned away from sleep. But he had found the babies in her place, the first two in a dumpster near the Thrift-Rite grocery store in town, the two together twisted close, potato-heads and flipper-arms down in among the paper and the fruit too ripe to sell. The feeling flashed again, had turned up hot there in her eyes then settled down in glowing heat, their talking moving like a dream right to the slamming of the guest-house door.

"Then it's real lucky I come here, huh? Maybe you can take the baby."

"Maybe."

"'Cause I ain't doing like Copper says this time. I ain't doing that stuff no more. I thought I could but I can't. Medix got th'last one at three months. I still got nightmares over it. Two years ago an' it still gets me. Y'unnerstand what I'm sayin'?"

"Yes."

"Now—look—I don't want you thinkin' it's the money. Copper paid the bill back then an' he'd do it again. But y'see it's diff'rent this time—he wanted 'em to clean me out for good. Make sure it won't happen no more. To protect my career, he said. An' he said he'd take care of all of it. Said he really needs me for the ac/dc gang—I'm a ac/dc star, he said—said there ain't nobody can get 'em like I can. 'No damn deal, ' I said—an'—then it got a lil' rough—"

"He hit you?"

"Well not much. Not a whole lot. Oh—y'know, couple to th'head an' all. But flat-handed like he always does. Nothin' in th'belly though. Not this time. I didn't give him no chance for that—"

Parker had tried to look away, to focus on the box again or on the door, to pull out from the eyes and glowing warm that rolled along her words and held him like the first two babies did when he had got them free. He could not then or now imagine Copper striking her.

"And that's when you ran?"

"No—I pre-tended I was hurt wors'n I was—I'm real good at that stuff—scare myself sometimes. I got him worried good. He even took me to the bathroom an' left me long enough to get out the window and solid gone. Right into the woods."

She had laughed a little wheezy laugh and rubbed the shawl-cape smooth upon her lap. Parker had shut his eyes, the warm still there but not so covered up with things he'd rather stayed outside. Martha was dead and the babies had kept bobbing up like toadstools in the spring and nothing else was half so real and true. Not County Home and preachers eating in a smack and crunch of lips and teeth. Not all the darkness he had passed among and changing times that left a stench upon the air. Not even what was growing out beyond his gates and inching closer year by year in flashing color clear across the sky. And he had sat there praying for the sound of Big Nurse knocking on the door.

"He—he must be pretty bad."

"Who? Copper?"

"Yes."

"Oh not so bad. Not bad as some I've known. He can be real sweet when he wants to. An' he pays good. Better'n most of the jerks I've worked for. No—he ain't so bad. He just don't know how it is this time—how—how I just can't do it this time."

"The abortion?"

"Yeah—that. An' the rest of it. I—I just can't do it."

"So you ran away?"

"Yeah—I was in them woods a long time—seemed like hours an' hours—what time is it now?"

"Must be nearly five."

"That all?"

"Yes."

"Well it seemed like I was out there a couple days. It was real dark too. Cold an' dark an' stinking like it gets on Sunday nights—y'know how that is—"

"Yes."

"An' then—then I seen the pa-trol comin'—"

"The Strip Police?"

"Them an' th'Beaver's security—th'B-Boys, Copper calls 'em. An' their lights was bright—brighter'n anything—like lookin' full at th'sun bright. They was in th'woods back of me—back where I first run in—"

"And they chased you?"

"What?"

"Did they chase you? The Police?"

"Oh—no. No, they never even seen me. I was raised in the country. My daddy thought I was a boy, I guess, till I started pokin' through. I was raised huntin' and fishin' and such—like you'd raise up a boy to do? We live back in th'Smokies—Tennessee—Big Bend of Reddies River. So buddies I never left no trail—I just booked it deep as I could get into them woods headin' north—an'—an' I was doin' ok till I fell."

"That's how you scraped your knees? How your dress got ripped?"

And there had been a silence then and rustling sounds and Parker slowly opened up his eyes. But nothing much had changed, the shawl-cape fluffed a bit and fuller on her thighs.

"I didn't even see that damn log—I hit my shins—went down pretty hard too. Right by your fence out there. The place with th'hole in it? You think maybe a coon made that hole?"

But Big Nurse had come up at last, her knock a loud one on the door then bustling inside not at all like she had done when numbers nine and ten had got away. The girl had stood up slowly, feathers catching on the shawl-cape in the front and several spinning free down in a spiral to the floor. And they had gone together to the guest-house, Big Nurse with an arm around the girl, the pathway crunching underfoot and air turned colder than before and everything feeling wet and sharp and salt-tinged from the east. From where the big ships labored through the ocean's rise and fall, their sound a moan of horn come long and muffled on the rising wind. Parker followed just a little ways behind, the girl's head hooded and the feathers dancing with each step and Big Nurse strong beside, a guide and help on through the central courtyard's yellow light. The wards had all been quiet as they passed, not one face showing in the windows there, not one face close against the special glass with lips and nose pressed flat and looking like a fish. He had felt the babies sleeping deep and sound in a warming-time before the dawn. And then the girl had joined them he was sure, in sleep like all the others down beneath the blankets Big Nurse always tucked in snug.

The fire was burning low when Parker got back to his room, the check on Gemma-Girl and Jesse-Lee a quick one in and out and a hurried note about the fence to Emment on the job-board as he left. The sunlight was almost there by then and sleep not hardly worth the effort it would take to let it come. So he stretched out instead in robe and slippered feet down in the old reclining chair and watched the pop and crackle of the dying fire, the spray and flash of sparkles on the deep soot back behind, a warm and feathered twisting there in spiral-dance upon the chimney ash.

CHAPTER TWO

Parker could hear the Firstlight Singing, not yet awake himself but on the fringes of it, dream-caught in a place he'd been before. The swamp in mist and eagle-cries above him in a distance real enough to touch. And then the music filtered in.

Sing to de day—sing day!
Sing day sing day sing day!

His eyes felt itchy, lids gone heavy and the corners stuck together hard. The singing sounded better than it usually did, more joined together verse by verse and not so ragged when the last words finally came. The blanket was a big one and the fire was crackling strong and warming out beyond his slippered feet. Emment must have come by on his way to eat.

To de lub lub lub!
To de good good good!
Sing glow-ree—glue-ree!

The Singing had been something Big Nurse started years ago, with just the older babies at first, the braver ones with two legs each and mouths that always worked, a little something extra for them when they finished up their meal. But now they nearly every one would sing, or wanted to and tried to do it, even those who lived in silence all the other hours of the day, in rolling-chairs or litter-bound and carried by the volunteers, on crutches or like Gemma-Girl and Jesse-Lee together hopping like a frog, they all would get there somehow for the rising of the sun. Parker stretched and yawned and listened to the voices rise and fall, the fire a pop and hiss among the words and steady down below.

Sing glow-ree
to the Lub Lub Lub!
Sing glue-ree
to de Goood!

It was Monday now, the thought almost a blow come in to jangle up the song and cut right through the blanket-warm and smoky fireplace heat. The final day for answering the men in suits, the lawyer and his little friend who came to see him just two weeks ago. They had wanted his thirty acres for a casino, a long talk then out front, along the fence and on the upper drive and finally at the gate itself beside their black and shiny car.

"You will never get a better offer, Mr. Sledge." The lawyer had pinkish rolls of fat beneath his chin and full red lips and bullfrog eyes that bulged behind his glasses sometimes blue and sometimes green. "The Sporus Group is top-flight all the way. Top dollar as well as that 'little extra' that makes for good feelings all around when it finally gets signed and done." He had blinked both eyes each time he stopped for breath.

"They want to put up a casino? Here?"

"Yes sir, they most certainly do. Sporus Georgia. Something like the one in Richmond but bigger. Bigger even than the ones in Waco and Little Rock. Probably an Egyptian theme. Pyramids. A sphinx or two. Real pretty. Especially all lit up at night."

"Egyptian?"

"Yes sir. Now that's just a guess on my part. Mr. Cibber here can better speak to that sort of thing. I'm land-acquisition mostly."

"It may be Sumerian-Revival, Mr. Shadwell." The second man had seemed a short and slender boy, black fuzz across his upper lip and hiding in the shadow of a nose that looked to be too big a thing for easy comfort on his face. "The final decision has not come down as yet."

"Yes yes. To be sure. But whatever it is you can bank on one thing, Mr. Sledge," he had rubbed at his chin with bloated, reddish fingers, "it will be a real asset to the State of Georgia."

"They might just go with the Neo-Bavarian, however." Mr. Cibber had seemed to notice his nose was there and tapped and tugged it side to side. "But probably not. Not so soon after that Hasidic mess in Jerusalem. Now everyone's entitled to their opinion, of course, but I personally feel very very strongly that—"

"Yes yes—but that's of no interest to Mr. Sledge, eh? No indeed. No, Mr. Sledge looks like a man who knows his business—a man who, if you will pardon my bluntness, knows how to deal. Isn't that right, Mr. Sledge?" He had made his eyes bulge larger then and scrunched his lips into a pucker like he meant to whistle or to blow. The sun had started in to peep and hide among the clouds.

"Deal?"

"Right right, Mr. Sledge. You have our proposal. You've heard all the fabulous plans—the Sporus Dream-Vision for South Georgia. It's all there. Open and in the light of day. All except the land. Everything is set to go but—"

"It will come down to Egyptian or Sumerian-Revival. One or the other, I think." Mr. Cibber had given up on his nose and begun to trouble the lip-fuzz instead, rubbing at it with short sweeps of a tiny index finger.

"Whatever is finally decided will be just fine with Mr. Sledge, Mr. Cibber, I'm sure of it. He looks like a man who appreciates beauty wherever he finds it. Yes. A definite lover of beauty." The eyes had seemed to blink in rhythm, first one and then the other as the sun came out to stay. "And a healthy profit as well, eh? But—hey' don't rush into anything is my advice. Just go over everything carefully. Let your accountant take a microscope to it. You'll see. We have positively nothing to hide. The offer speaks for itself. And what it plainly says is: 'A healthy profit for Mr. Parker Sledge!' Eh?"And he had patted Parker's back and left the papers with him and had promised to return in two weeks' time.

Parker pushed down on the chair and sat up, the blanket slipping to the floor. The voices outside were about to stop, the song already lasting longer than was usual for a Monday. The meeting was for two o'clock and Parker rubbed his chin and shuffled toward the bathroom door, feathers floating from the dust to catch and hold the blanket as he passed.

CHAPTER THREE

The girl's voice surprised him, seeming closer than it was as if she somehow floated on the dancing dust and sparkling motes, appearing there inside his only chicken-house without him seeing her at all. Sunlight was streaming in most everywhere, from cracks above his head the strongest of the rest, in shafts both thin and fat come down to give the air a place to shine. The day was warmer than it started out to be, the sun bright-cutting through what breeze was left and giving off a feel of summertime. He had been sitting close beside the broken feeders ever since the second meeting with the Sporus-Men had ended in a squeal of tires and gravel spinning out behind their car. The girl herself appeared in the doorway, her features darkened by the sunlight strong behind her as she stepped slowly onto the sawdust floor. She came into a better focus at the feed-sacks, stopping there in the shade, the shawl-cape and the feathers gone and someone's sweater and a yellow jumper in their place.

"I been out walking—this is sure some place y'got here."

"Yes. Are you feeling better?"

"A whole lot. Ya'll eat good here."

The Sporus-Men, Lawyer Shadwell and Mr. Cibber, had driven to the central courtyard, let in by Emment who had phoned to tell him they were on their way. And he had stood there talking with them till the Fresh-Air bell had rung. Lawyer Shadwell had seemed nervous from the very first.

"This—this is quite an extensive complex you have

here, Mr. Sledge."

"Yes. It's grown a lot."

"Please forgive my obvious surprise—but—but no one told us it was quite this—well—um—big." Lawyer Shadwell had kept licking his lips and looking right to left as if he expected someone to suddenly spring out and make everything shrink down to his expectations.

"Very nice brickwork—modified neo-Savannah with just the barest touch of Proto-Memphis. Beautiful cornices. They look like Stuart and Early—did you use them?" Mr. Cibber's voice had made Lawyer Shadwell twitch and fumble with his tie.

"Look, Mr. Sledge." Shadwell had moved in close, his hand come down on Parker's shoulder in a gentle squeeze and pat. He smelled of fish. "Look—I wasn't told how big it was—all these buildings—fences—is that a corral over there? Do you raise horses?" He had stepped back and frowned, fingers clasping once or twice in air before they found the pockets of his vest.

"No. No horses. We had a pony once but it wandered off. Toward Macon, we think."

"Yes—well—not a thing was said about all this. The Sporus-Group usually checks out these matters long before they send us in—so—listen, what I'm trying to say is that I don't think any demolition work was figured into the initial offer and—"

"Demolition work?"

"—the initial offer will have to be adjusted accordingly. Oh my yes it will. Did you understand the Tentative Agreement Clause? It might cover some of the necessaries but that would, of course, depend entirely on which of the multiple-options you decided to choose."

"Multiple what?"

"Options. They're usually on page fifty-six—the yellow sheet in that packet I left with you? No, of course not. What am I thinking? The options are in Form 310X. Your packet as I remember it was a standard 40P40. Somebody," he had chuckled out a cough-like sound and scratched his head, "certainly messed up on this one, didn't they? I mean, that should be rather obvious by now, don't you think? Yes indeed. And—I'll be totally frank here—I just don't know what to do. I mean, God, you must have five, ten buildings back here—big—brick."

"Some of that brick can be saved though." Mr. Cibber had licked his lips and rubbed at his nose. "That's Royal Oglethope there on the front steps. And White Talmadges holding the railing. Imitations obviously, but nicely done all the same."

"We," Shadwell had nudged Mr. Cibber and cleared his throat loudly a few times, "we were led to believe that this was a chicken farm. Oh—we were informed that you sometimes took in strays as well—but no one said a word about all this—this—brick."

"I used to do that."

"Pardon?"

"Chickens. I used to raise them. But they're all gone now."

"Do you mind if I take a closer look?" Mr. Cibber's nose had seemed to be leading him to the right, toward the Recreational Hall where Big Nurse and the volunteers were inside teaching all the Two-Hands how to button up their shirts. "Mr. Sledge?"

"What?"

"The Neo-Savannah? May I take a closer look?"

"Oh—sure. Sure—that's fine."

"Then you don't raise chicken's any more?" Mr. Shadwell had tugged at his tie and then his vest and glared at Mr. Cibber skipping quickly toward the nearest wall.

"Chickens?" Parker had watched as Mr. Cibber pushed in through the hedges to the wall, beside the steps, his hands begun almost immediately to rub and feel his way out around the corner toward the concrete wheelchair ramp.

"Yes—you aren't in the chicken business now, you say?"

"No. No, I gave that up a long time ago. People kept coming out here at all hours of the night and stealing them. I used to have ten thousand."

"People stole the chickens?"

"Yes. And that's why I put in a fence. Not the same one we have now. Another one. Years ago. But that didn't stop nothing. Chickens can fly, y'know?"

"No. I didn't realize they—'

"Oh—nothing fancy. Short-haul stuff mostly. Y'see—people'd break into the houses and set loose more'n they got. And the loose ones'd all take off flying. Like I said—nothing fancy—not very far at a time—but high enough and long enough eventually to beat it over my fence and wind up in a gator's belly or laid out flat as a board on Freedom Highway. I got tired of it. Only took me five years to get there too. I don't even eat chicken now. That was a long time ago. When I worked with Capstone Poultry. Before they got ate up by Yakimama Foods. Anyways—before all this. Before I changed direction."

"Then—is this," Mr. Shadwell had waved his hand to take in most of the buildings, "a boarding school? It certainly looks like a school. Feels like a school. It has that kind of feeling about it. Oh my. I fear the Zoning Board provided us a rather fuzzy picture of your present status. That's more than apparent by just looking around. Yes indeed. More than apparent. A Mr.—Mr. Peacock, I think it was—Chairman of the County Commission—right? Yes. Well he personally seemed to think that you were mostly still in the chicken business out here."

"Well—he hasn't been 'out here' very much. I can't even remember the last time. No. No chickens. Not any more. Never again. That's all behind me now."

"I see. Then it must be the other thing—the strays? Is that it?"

"Strays?'

"Uh yes—the children. And others. I'm sorry but this is so embarrassing." He had swallowed hard and tugged his tie knot down below the second roll of fat. "You see, I have absolutely no control whatsoever over the preliminary research. And neither does Mr. Cibber. That sort of thing is dealt with by the Regional Office—Richmond for the South Atlantic. Our responsibility is closing details—transfer of cash payments—acquisition—plants-and-grounds overview and cost-estimates—those sorts of things. And in my nearly twenty years with Sporus, it's always proceeded absolutely without complication. Of course, Georgia is new territory for us—and—well—look," he had started to pat Parker's shoulder again but changed his mind mid-reach, "I just need to know your decision. The Regional Office can work out the details with you. The decision is the main thing anyway. Yes. The rest will sort out in due season. Yes?"

"Decision?"

"Right. The proposal—it's in those papers I left with you—the packet? The standard 40P40?"

"Oh. I never read them."

"What?" His eyes had widened, touched with sunlight through his glasses to a green as pale as springtime grass. "What did you say?"

"I'm not selling."

"What?"

And then the Fresh-Air bell had rung and one long piercing scream had brought the lawyer's eyes to blue and back again to green and somewhere in between the two before they locked in full and wide on Mr. Cibber scrambling like a crab around the corner bricks and up and down upon the sidewalk with the Two-Hands babies and the One-Eyes too, close on his heels and reaching for them in a sweep of flapping fingers in the air, and others right behind, the Hoppers and Gemma-Girl and Jesse-Lee and Fun-Heads butting at the volunteers and Big Nurse bringing up the rear and pushing out the Rolling-Carts that always left the pavement for the shrubs, all come together in a chirping, clucking, rumble-roar of joy to be outside again at last. The car had scattered gravel everywhere and Mr. Cibber made a sound like "gak" the only thing that Parker heard him say.

The girl was sitting on the driest feed sack, long hair down in shiny strands upon her shoulders and her wide eyes pointed at the nearest shaft of light.

"It looks like little fish."

"Pardon?"

"Them things in the light. Swimming up and down. Like fish. I used t'think they was air-fish. In my Daddy's barn. That's what I called 'em anyways. Air-fish. Was they here about me?" She crossed her ankles and smoothed the jumper down over her knees.

"What?"

"Them men I saw—was they lookin' for me?"

"No—no, they were here for something else."

"They sure did leave in some kind a hurry, didn't they? That lil' one nearly didn't make it in the car. Them kids 'bout made him stay. You see that?"

"Yes."

"I seen most a the kids here. Got took all over. This mornin' after bre'fast. Man oh man, you folks eat good."

"You're feeling better you say?"

"Oh yeah. Much. You got you some nice people here. Seem kinda nervous sometimes. But nice. Especially that big ol' nurse—Miss Pecks? She was real sweet though. Let me use her shower."

"Yes. She's a good one."

"An' them other ladies—they work real hard—"

"Yes. Volunteers."

"Well they was all real nice. Like Miss Pecks."

"Yes. We don't get as many volunteers any more. Mostly just a few nuns now."

"Nuns? Like the Cath'lics have?"

"Yes. I'm not sure why they come. But we don't ask many questions."

"Yeah. I saw that. Nobody really asted me nothin'.

Y'know—nothin' real personal. Just smiled a lot. Helped me settle in. Course, I made up the difference—never have known how to keep it shut—not for long anyways. You saw that last night f'yourself—"

"Yes."

He had wanted very much to be alone, to think and watch the dancing fish and try to look ahead to what he knew was forming out beyond the boundaries of his land. But she was settling in to stay awhile, the feeling of it word by word and reaching out to touch him through the brittle light.

"An' you—you're Mr. Sledge?"

"Yes."

"Then you built this place, didn't you?"

"Yes."

"How'd you ever get into somethin' like this? Nobody seemed to know. Not for sure anyways." She laughed, the sound an echo from before the chair and eagle-dream. "I know I know—I ast a lot of questions."

"Yes."

"But you can't never find out nothin' if you don't ast, y'know?"

"Yes."

"Them kids—they—"

"Yes?"

"Who they belong to?"

CHAPTER FOUR

The question reached him softly, almost as a whisper out across the stillness of the chicken house, the girl then moving to a place where sunlight pushed down strong upon her head. Her hair had sparkled there, the little fish a whirl about her sometimes glittered in their swimming through the dusty air. And he had answered her, not really wanting to but somehow feeling trapped, reciting like a schoolboy stiff and slow, the words not even half of what was left unsaid and rolling out upon a tumbling crash and bump of time, of years behind and things unfolding now and soon to show themselves within the pain of choice and action yet to come. He told her bits and pieces of the past. The safest way and for the moment surest in the sticking end-to-end and side-to-side that held the flow of moments like the patches of a much-used quilt. He told her what had happened in the past.

"They left you? Your parents?"

"Yes—at what used to be the County Home."

"An orphanage?"

"Yes. It used to be near the water-front—the docks—down where the beltway and the Mall are now."

"I been there. It's pretty. On Sunday night especially. When the wind's blowin' right. I used t'go there after my last show. Drive down and park and watch the people. It's open twenty-four hours, y'know?"

"It looked different then—big oaks and dogwoods—magnolia trees—the building was brick—deep red—"

And as he watched her stretch her legs and fold her arms in front, down on the yellow cloth that seemed to rise up easy with her breathing, iron bed and windows lived again a flicker in her eyes and pursing of her lips, a nod of head and tumble-down of black black hair among the tiny golden fish. He wanted to but couldn't seem to stop the words from coming out.

"I was eight-years-old."

"When they left you?"

"Yes."

"Ever see 'em again?"

"No. They couldn't make it together—neither of them. I remember some of that. A little of it toward the end. My father was the first to leave." And then his mother took him to the Home, one steamy afternoon in August with a storm off rumbling toward the north, his clothes inside a canvas bag and one last hug before she left. That night the storm had made the shutters bang and groan against the windows up above his head, the other boys asleep and lightning flashes streaking every wall with shafts of dark that lingered when he shut his eyes. He had stayed there two days shy of ten long years.

"Then you left? After high school?"

"Yes."

"God I wish I could a done that. They give you a diploma?"

"Yes."

"God I wish I had one. I run off after seventh grade."

But he had stayed in Carver City, in the town at first in furnished rooms and then in one old farm-house near the Swamp, had worked in anything he could and saved his money week by week until he had enough to buy up land nobody else would have.

"So you wasn't in Viet Nam?"

"No. I never went."

"I thought you might of been—most guys—most—"

"My age?"

"Yeah. But hey—wait—I didn't mean—I just hear a lot about it—in my work. I sometimes wonder what it was like. Shoot, I guess I seen all them movies. Some a them twice. Course, I like 'Rambo' the best. You ever seen any a them?"

"No."

"Well I like them the best. Must a been real bad over there, don't y'think?"

"Yes."

But they had turned him down the four times that he tried to go, his heart not sounding right and something else gone wrong he never thought about again. And so he stayed at home and worked instead and watched the changes come, the TV-Negroes mostly, joining in an almost rhythmic way across the nightly news, the distant Blacks that marched and sang and bled and settled in to take their rest once they could sit down with the Whites in school and café booth, on bus and in the depot too, in movie-house and ballpark, safe and snug their freedom close about them law-tight and directive-bound a prize that always seemed to him too slight a thing for proper ending to it all. And that sad burning-time he read about and watched as flicker on his television screen had not come near enough to see, not coming even to the Sutter County line, not as a lynching or a blazing cross or long-haired howling at the rising of the war. Though the other things had come in while he worked, the local ordinances pushed through by the pound it sometimes seemed, no resting space back then to do much more than wonder at their bud and blossom: marriage chapels first out on the southern fringes of the town, and then the Home torn down and waterfront and shopping centers quickly turned to malls, two and three to serve the naval bases further down the coast and all the new-hired labor pouring in to work the shiny factories the Germans and the Japanese had built, the county changing more and more, in seafood and in real estate, the corporation shrimp fleets and the condo clutter of the beach, the northern bankers and the textile marts, and all this like so much plowed ground for the last to come and finally push aside the rest, the strip clubs and the lingerie and condom chains, abortion clinics and the specialty hotels and motels and the law firms that promised a divorce in one day's time, and fetal-tissue labs and acres of human reproduction waste-disposal plants and the Medix Corporation sucking everything it seemed inside its ever-growing promise of a better life.

But before it all clamped fully down, before the State rose up with licenses to let inside most everything from Abortion Pride Parades to mobile fetal-waste-disposal units giving discount coupons up and down the Georgia coast—just before it all was legalized and settled in to stay, he bought his land and worked it into shape right through the ripening time of what had steadily grown up strong out just beyond his gate and fences. With something new sure now to come back on him when the lawyer and his little friend had time to rest and think.

Watching the girl lick her lips and begin a smile that

seemed to drop away almost as soon as he noticed, Parker thought of that final step, the one that made it sure no peace would ever come again. The Governor, "Catfish" Bebber's face still clear in mind as when it came up on the TV screen back there when everything had still been mostly local. But after all those years of steady building, finally, a formal edict, an executive order arose from the pleas of local politicians and the Chamber of Commerce, Governor Bebber himself its author, giving everything the seal of his own approval in his own words—as he signed it amidst the flash and whir of cameras and the cheers of his lieutenants. The face and words burned deeply into Parker's memory, there again whenever he gave more than passing thought to everything out past his fencing and his gate. The face had been sweating in the bright lights. But the voice was deep and sure there on the birthday of a tourism more lucrative than any theme park could ever make come true.

"Folks're gonna do what folks do. I'm not in favor of all this personally, y'unnerstand—but, I'm a Governor, not a Preacher—so we're carving out these places so's we can keep it under control. Keep it clean and safe."

And the smile had lasted a full minute, big teeth showing bright while he handed out the souvenir pens. And when it was all done, there were four carved-out, tax-supported, "Reproductive Safe Zones" down along the Georgia coast with neon sometimes seen from miles at sea.

"So you raised chickens?" The smile stayed longer this time, her voice beginning to sound more relaxed.

"Yes. For a few years. I had ten houses like this

one."

"Daddy had some chickens. We never ate none of 'em though. He just liked to have 'em around, I guess. To watch 'em. I hated them chickens. Even the eggs tasted funny t'me."

"I didn't raise them very long." Until a month or two before his wife had run off with a sailor or some salesman she had met, the man himself a blurry profile in the car he drove to pick her up out where she went to meet him when she thought that Parker was asleep. He had known how things had turned, two years or so into what hurt him still to think about, the marriage nearly empty then but warmth beside him in the night, a soothing thing and hard to give away. He heard that she had died a year or so past when he took the first two babies in.

"You was married?"

"Yes. Five years."

"Funny—but you don't look like the marryin' kind—an' I seen 'em all, b'lieve me. You just don't look like no married guy. What happened? Divorce?"

"No—we never divorced—not that I know about anyway. She left."

"Yeah. I know how that can be. Happened t'me once. Fool split an' then called from Canada no less t'say he'd take care of it. The divorce? Pay all th'expenses, y'know? Didn't do it though. I found out when I applied for my workin' papers."

"Working papers?"

"Y'know—Carnal Services License—the CSL? State and Fed'ral B-Girl Papers? Or whatever in hell they're calling 'em this month."

"I—oh. Yes. Yes I—" A Bebber-special, part of what

came rolling out once the executive order settled in to stay. To link up with the national laws and directives. Everything neat and locked down tight.

"Damned fool hadn't done a thing. Nothin' on record—even in Canada. An' you can't get you no license when you're married 'less your spouse signs. An' then he gets him a straight ten per-cent for doin' nothin'—no shit—that's the law buddies. So I had to file—costed me three hundred dollars an' some change. So you can't tell me nothin' I don't a'ready know about that runnin' off scam. No sir. She ever write?"

"What?"

"Your wife. She ever write or anythin'?"

"No."

"Well it's better that way. My ex still writes. Wantin' money mostly. Yours didn't go in for th'chickens huh? That what done it?"

"I—I think so. In part."

"She give you any kids?"

"No—no she—"

"Not even a nibble? Not in five years?"

"No—we—"

"I know I know—Condom City, huh? Pills? NoFuss shots maybe? I know how it is. I don't do no more shots though. You can lose y'hair doin' NoFuss. I seen it happen. Them new clinics're real big on it but—I just—I—" She brushed back her hair and ran her fingers gently across the ridge of her nose, fingertips dabbing at her cheeks and dropped down slowly to her lap to scratch her other hand. Her hair seemed covered up by tiny fish. "Well you sure got you a bunch a inneresting kids now though, don't you? You like 'em better'n the chickens?" The smile was shaky, jagged in a trembling way that made her words sound shrill. She bowed her head and reached to wipe away her tears. "I—I'm sorry—I hadn't oughta said—look, I'm just messed up right now—but I'll get better—better'n this—I'm just messed up—"

He had wanted very much to get up from his place and move the few feet through the light and dancing fish to touch and hold her there, just to sit close by her in the shaft of light and tell her how it was back in the darkness after Martha left. To tell her how the babies had begun to push it all away and two-by-two and one-by-one to bring back everything he lost but warmth beside him in the night. But she had wiped her cheeks and smiled and smoothed her hair behind her ears and let him take her further on along the surface of the things that he had done.

"A dumpster? You found the first ones in a dumpster?"

And he had told her of the two, their cries like baby rats past where he parked his truck, the weekly shopping done and more from habit than from need since Martha went away. The cries had gotten louder when he climbed up on the dumpster and looked in.

"And they was just layin' there? In the trash?"

"Yes. Two of them."

"I heard about stuff like that—stories—how it was. Still happens sometimes, I guess—clinics messing up—I seen that a few times too. On the television. Though it must have been a whole lots worse back then."

"Yes."

He had had to dig and pull among the rotting fruit to

get them free, their flipper-arms about him then and holding to his neck and chest, their mouths thick slits with flaps of skin that plopped and puckered when they cried, a buzzing clack of sound there too like tree-frogs calling out for rain.

"An' nobody else would take 'em in?"

"That's right. I hadn't planned on doing it myself. The—the clinics were new then and the law—the new law had just been passed. This was fifteen years ago remember—and nobody was sure who had jurisdiction. They—they weren't exactly pretty babies and they were—they seemed sick."

"Couldn't th'clinics put 'em to sleep back then? Like now? Like what they do now?"

"That was the thing—nobody seemed to know. The laws were new—the Directives—and the clinics had only just come in—a few at first. Way back toward where the Waterfront Mall is now. Nobody seemed to know what to do. The churches—not a one had any more room—not here—"

"So you just took 'em in yourself?"

"Yes. I did it. I knew a nurse. From high school—"

"That big woman that took me all around? That Miss Pecks?"

"Yes. She came to help me that first night—I phoned her and she came. And stayed."

"Did they live?"

"What?"

"Them first ones—did they live?"

"Yes—they were just hungry. They're still here. You might have seen them—they work in the garden and help out in the kitchen. We call them Bo and Peep."

The girl was frowning down toward where her feet pushed into shade, the shaft of light stopping there like a stocking just above her purple shoes. Those first two babies had grown taller than he thought they would and in their growing somehow pulled in more, all kinds and found beyond the fence and living off the land, swamp-hoppers and the crawling ones with shoulders bigger than their heads, the prowlers in the woods beyond the bright lights on the Strip, afraid and only slowly made to take the food and blankets that he brought and slower yet to give up on the cold and dark and come to live inside. And some had been dropped off and bundled tight against the fence or at the gate and then as time went by and others came to help—Emment and the volunteers in answer to a story here and there, a feature in a paper that some church had run or late-night television show—the paid-for babies (that their families wouldn't tend or couldn't bear to see) began to come and sprinkle in among the rest with monthly rates to keep them every one in food and shoes and clothes to wear.

"And church people gave you money?"

"Just at first. In the beginning. Two big grants for the building we needed to do. Sometimes donations still come in. Not so many any more. Not since the new laws settled in. But right at first the churches helped a lot. Helped us build a home out here. I tore down the coops—the chicken houses right off. All but this one. We store things in it—back there. The grants helped build the Wards and Recreation Hall. The Dining Hall. The Honor Barn was already there. We fixed it up though. New roof and insides. Did you see it?"

"Yeah. She took me everywhere."

"The Big Boys live there now."

"Yeah—I seen 'em. They're big ok. One looked near eight foot—that red-head with the pointy ears?"

"Eric. Yes. He was tiny when he came in. They all were. Most have families."

"And they send 'em here?" She shook her head and let the hair bounce down upon her cheeks, the shaft of light grown dimmer now, less fish to swim upon her dress, her legs in shade from knees to shoes.

"Yes."

The chicken-house was quiet like the calming in the air before a summer rain, a stillness there that made him want to close his eyes and sleep. Her voice was nearly hoarse and with a touch of sadness in it that he hadn't heard before, a child-like reaching out across the light and swimming fish, a difference somehow real enough to hold. But nothing that she said came clear, the words almost a humming through the stillness near at hand. Soon it would be time for EveningSing, his time to wear a funny hat and help the babies make the sun go down. He loved to see them then the most, close-packed together out before the Dining Hall, their music helping day-by-day to keep the hurt of Martha well away. But this time he would rather hear the girl, her words enough to bring him sleep and dreams of eagles soaring to their nesting-tree, in feathered blur against the darkening sky and trilling cry near lost upon a rising wind. Her voice had broken through to where the babies ran to find the light, his own fear open to the dusty air and Sporus-Men among the shadows now and calling for the fences one-by-one to fall. And then he heard her plain.

"How many you got?"

"What?"

"Kids—how many are there in here?"

"Four hundred. They tell me that anyway. The last report. I've never counted them myself."

And she had laughed and got up quickly in a blur of fish and shadows speckled on her dress, her hair dropped to her shoulders in a bounce and splay that reached across her neck to touch her chin. Her fingers felt like fire upon his cheeks, a pressure lifting him to stand, above her half a head or more, and look down into eyes so wide it made him ache to breathe. Her belly pressed into him, soft and fitting slow and careful there and she had kissed him just a little touch and bowed her head and helped him hold her in the fading light.

CHAPTER FIVE

Nothing much but yellow-flies were biting and his favorite place was choked in mist, the air gone heavy and the water dark and slicked and slimy to the touch. The weather had turned warm with rain and then a clearing sky and breezes suited more to spring than fall. The girl, Judy Taylor, was with him in the boat. A week had passed since he had met her at the door. Big Nurse had told him that and asked him what he planned to do. Just this morning. After breakfast in the Dining Hall, the babies loud behind them then, shrieks and hopping thumps and little squeals among the clack of rolling chairs and shuffling feet. Not one had made a nighttime break since Gemma-Girl and Jesse-Lee. Big Nurse had brushed off bits of egg and bacon from her apron as she talked.

"A week, Mr. Sledge—that's how long it's been. We've acted cordial. Like we always do. We've let her come and go. I even took her on the tour. Personally. You never said to do otherwise, so we did it like we always do." She had hung her head and cleared her throat and then looked back at him with just a trace of red come out to spread across her cheeks and mostly stay. "Look, this isn't none of my business—I know that—you're a grown man. But it's causing trouble—"

"Trouble?"

"Yes—with the volunteers mostly. But it's really everybody. You know what she is."

"She dances—she told me what she does."

But more, much more than that had come out slowly late at night, beside her in the dark or half-light from the flames, down on the pallet that he used when she was with him in his room, the fireplace bright with sparkles then and glowing logs that hissed the smoke up quick into the black. They had talked together every night, for hours when he finished EveningSing and his rounds and read the bedtime story at the Big Boys' Honor Barn, every night inside the Guest House or back in his room together close and touching, a kiss sometimes before she slept and blankets tucked in warm around her on the bed. She had told him many things.

"Mr. Sledge—she—she's a B-Girl—she—"

"Yes. I know that. She told me that."

"She—she's been that way for years. Working for—for them—the Strip people—for years—"

"Yes. She told me that. The ac/dc gang—"

"Beg pardon?"

"She told me what she used to do."

The story coming slowly in the pop and hiss of fire, the shadows in a flicker on her face and out about her on the floor, a little girl again and fearful of the mountain dark, the twisted smile there on her father's face and other men a whiskey-smell among the laurel and the pine, the fear alive and grown too big to hold inside—a breaking free then and the lonesome of the road alone and traveling south toward lights that kept the dark away.

"Well—well she's—she's clean at least. She has papers. I checked. I saw them while she was showering. They're all in order. Marked A-I just two weeks ago."

"Clean?"

"No positive testing—if the State Lab can still be

trusted."

"Yes. She has her working-papers. I knew that too."

Ten years gone by a breathing time or two in telling how they passed, the whiskey-smell and stench of burning whirling through the dance, in muted light that filled with smoke and twisted smiles on faces down below her stage. And babies lost and gone before they even opened up their eyes and tried to see.

"It's good that she's clean. That's something to be grateful for."

"Grateful?"

"Look, Mr. Sledge—I generally don't bring you much in the way of personal problems. I don't bother you with that. I just take care of things. Just like I have for fifteen years. Truth is we don't have many problems as a rule—very few from the permanents—Emment, Cook Crundle, Bo and Peep, Doc and my own people. They don't listen to talk—they don't let it bother them. And they don't usually cause any." She had frowned and then let her face begin to relax, almost in stages, head slowly shaking from side to side, eyes wide and her breathing loud enough to hear. "But the volunteers've always needed extra attention. Careful handling. They seem to scare easier. I don't know why. Maybe it's because they don't stay long enough to understand how things are around here. Y'know. How even when we sometimes mess-up, it doesn't necessarily mean that the outsiders're going to—"

"Mess-up?"

"Well yes. Like Emment sometimes does. The whiskey. The places in town—or out yonder on the Strip."

"Emment? Whiskey?"

"You—you mean you didn't know?"

It somehow seemed a foreign thing, the words not fitting what he saw in Emment day-by-day, a picture of him down among the smoke and muted light and twisted smiles not holding there for Parker even when he tried to make it form and stay. Big Nurse had blinked her eyes and looked away.

"I—I'm sorry—I—I thought you knew."

"No."

"Well its' been a long time now since he's done any of that. Not a mess-up in nearly five years. And it wasn't much even then. Drunk and disorderly. Nothing too serious. Nothing bad enough to go to Court. And nothing else came of it—in fact, nobody out there seemed to connect him with us at all."

"I see."

"But this is different, Mr. Sledge. The stories are—more—more vicious this time. More persistent and nasty. The volunteers told me—they do the shopping now and they hear things. And they know where she comes from and what can happen. Especially if people start believing what they hear. That the girl is diseased. That's one of the stories. There are others if you want to—"

"No."

"I tried to ignore it at first myself. But it's gotten beyond that. And last night a delegation from the volunteers came to see me. The two from the Sisters of Perpetual Vigilance—they were in Memphis during the madness—when the Presleyites nearly killed fourteen of the babies in the Delta Sanctuary. That home they had over there for addict-births? Sister Mary-Cindy saved four of them herself. The Sanctuary building was wrecked and—"

"There aren't any Presleyites here. Not in Sutter County."

"But it's starting out the same—can't you see that? The talk. It started with talk. They took in a Priscilla Second-Class, a priestess-trainee—a teenager—fourteen years old. Addicted to cocaine and God knows what else. She had run away from GraceLand. Pregnant. Like that girl. And rumors started flying—like here—it got ugly. Like it's getting here. The Presleyites thought the girl had been kidnapped—thought the Delta people had kidnapped her for her baby—for—for organ transplants. And then other priestesses disappeared—a few were Priscilla Unos, the choir singers. And then the King Creoles came to get them. In the middle of the night. No warning. They just came. Nearly a hundred of them. And wrecked Delta, Mr. Sledge. And took the girl away."

"It's not the same."

"Well the volunteers think it is. They're frightened. By the talk. By what they've seen and heard out there. The Strip Police. The rest of it. DIAL-A-BORT. Medix expansion. The new crematoriums. You know yourself how it's been going since Georgia first got those fetal waste disposal contracts. This whole end of the state. Worse and worse. The volunteers aren't used to it. Some—the younger ones especially—are already talking about leaving. And we need them, Mr. Sledge. Every one of them. Winter's coming on and there's no time to put out a call for more. There's no time for that. No time for training and—"

"What do you suggest we do?"

"Send her back. Right back where she came from. Right now. That's the only thing you can do."

"Send her back?"

And she had told him one more time before he left how talk was spreading like a water stain and everywhere at once, was mixing close with fear about the lawyer and his friend, and talk and fear then turning in a way she saw as clear as day hard toward the ending of the thing they both had worked so hard to build.

"She's trouble, Mr. Sledge. She can't stay here. She's pregnant and desperate and trouble. And she's one of them. One of them out yonder. The new kind. And they'll find out she's here. And maybe those other men'll use her. Somehow. To get this place away from you. And what'll these babies do then, Mr. Sledge? Where will they go?"

He had promised Judy that he'd come and get her when the babies left for class and play. He wanted her to see the swamp in early morning when the sun began to burn away the mist, down past the sawmill and the gator crawl, the broken cypress and the hummocks where the heron sometimes hid. He wanted her to see Old Sutter's Dock the most and where his castle used to stand, the little bluffs and twisted oaks and Spanish moss so long it nearly brushed the water when the air got still. And maybe see an eagle on the wing before the day was done. But Big Nurse made him late. Judy had opened up the Guest House door before he even knocked.

"I thought you maybe changed your mind."

"No. Something came up."

#

The boat was bobbing near the last pylons of the Dock, the ones Old Man Sutter sank in deep and hard to hold the weight his moonshine jugs put down. All gone away now but the last pylons poking through the water, bird-stained white upon a green that looked alive. They hadn't talked much until now, Judy dressed in Emment's extra overalls and Parker's newest flannel shirt, her hair thick-braided down her back. And they hadn't caught a single fish.

"You ok?"

She put her cane pole down, the tip poked out the flat-nosed bow and line gone slack and floating near the bob. Her face looked whiter somehow in the rolling mist, a spot of light at play across her hair. The sun was trying hard to burn on through, still trying like it had all morning with a dance of light that sped across the water always just beyond the chugging of the boat. And he had watched it come and go and tried to bring back the feeling close together with the babies back among their day.

"Yes. Just thinking."

"That can hurt. I've tried it an' I know."

Her laugh was like the light back then upon the water, there and gone to leave behind an almost echo of itself like what the words that Big Nurse spoke had done, to touch his own fear like a puff of air upon a glowing coal and bring up flames that danced in closer every day from where the lawyer and his friend had gone.

What'll these babies do then, Mr. Sledge?

Where will they go?

But when they finally tied up to the biggest pylon, the motor cut and nothing left to do but tell her that she'd have to go, he watched her fish instead and let the babies come and go and sing among the feeling then so strong, a binding there and close together and enough at last to hold them all, like bone and feathers muscled and alive, full wide and strong enough to soar. A burst of sunlight made her frown. And somewhere past the cypress and the oaks a scream of siren rose and fell.

"Let's go back now, Parker. It stinks here. Like a Sunday night. I don't like this place very much. Can we go back home?"

CHAPTER SIX—FRAGMENTS

-1-

Buster Welborne was working the third-shift PhoneBank and hadn't had a break all night. The Big Board kept on lighting up each time he thought it had settled down. Row on row and up and down just like a blinking Christmas tree. Hour after hour with the other boys too tired or dry-mouthed now to give the greeting Mr. Cutter taught them how to say. Buster was ready for a break. But Cutter never let up on his pacing out across the rows, so close behind sometimes the boys would jump when he went brushing by. The old man couldn't keep his belly inside the regulation shirt.

"Hello—yeah? Hello!"

Is—is this the—the Medix Hotline?

"What? Medix? No—no this is Dial-a-Bort Central Dispatch. You need some help?" Buster adjusted his headset, its tiny microphone bobbing a bit near his lips.

And there he was, old Cutter come up smack behind and leaning in to hear, his headset tilted a bit to one side. Buster tried to lick his lips and make the right words form and flow.

"May I help you, ma'am?"

"Is there a problem, Welborne?"

"Uh—oh no sir, Mr. Cutter—lady here seems to think we're—"

It ain't no rumor neither—my husband seen it for himself—it—it's all true—

"Ma'am—ma'am? This is Dial-A-Bort—the Medix number is—ma'am, if you'll just—"

Cutter always smelled like pickles in a jar, like how

it smelled each time the lid popped off and gave a tickle to your nose. Buster hated the smell and the red splotches on Cutter's cheeks, the little whirls of skin that looked like spiders' legs and the strands of hair near purple where they crossed. Up close the whole thing made him sick but payday was tomorrow and the money here was ten times better than that Medix shovel job he used to work his senior year at school. At that job he never got a single raise and wearing all that special gear had hurt his chest and back and sometimes, when a rush was on, the foreman worked them well past quitting time, the oven heat so bad his skin had come out blistered in the places where the gas-mask didn't reach. His cousin got him on with Dial-A-Bort six months ago. The lady on the other end was gasping in between her words. Leaning in with a blast of pickle smell, Old Cutter plugged into the auxiliary outlet and adjusted his headset. It became a three-way then.

—monsters—and they—they'll come spread—spread-ing—every-where—and they—they got B-Girls too—the—the ones—ones who ain't been passed—the sick ones—out there—it—it ain't no—rumor—

"Ma'am? Ma'am listen—"

"I'll take it, Welborne. There's been a royal screw-up somewhere. Just log in the time. In your book—there—right there—good. Lissen to me, Ma'am—can you hold it—I said, hold it!" The woman's voice snapped off like someone cut it with a knife. Old Cutter sounded like a snarling dog. "Lissen me, ma'am! Lissen now. This is not Medix. You hear me? Ma'am—I said, did you hear me?"

I—uh—I—I—

"This is Dial-A-Bort—the Medix number is RD-3131. Did you hear me, ma'am?"

Yes—yes—3131? Well ain't that what I dialed?

"No ma'am, I don't think so."

You're Dial-A-Bort you say?

"Yes ma'am. Perhaps we can help you with something?"

Oh—oh my—no—oh no—

Her laugh had made Buster's stomach pitch and roll, a cackle like a chicken tiny in his ears but reaching deep and buzzing as it mixed in with her words.

Oh no—no no no—oh my—not me—I—I'm sixty-five—Dial-A-Bort—hah! No—I seen your vans—them trucks y'have—I know what y'are—an' you ain't no help in this here. No sir you ain't!

"It's been the same all night, Mr. Cutter." Buster pushed down the microphone and whispered." No let up—second shift too—they told us—"

"I know all that already, Welborne." Cutter pushed his microphone to one side and shook his head. His voice was barely audible. "Just log her in. Has she given you her name?"

"No sir."

"Ma'am?" Cutter pushed the microphone up to his lips and spoke loudly. " Ma'am?"

I seen lots a things—I'm sixty-five, y'know—so I seen it all. I know what's real—I watch them medical shows—ever one. Now I know lots a people think it's all just talk—plague an' monsters too—all talk—but I know diff'rent—I know all about that monster bidness an' it ain't no talk—nosir—it's real—real as can be—an'—

"Ma'am—hold it a minute now will—"

My husband seen 'em on the Strip—in them woods back there—back toward that place—y'know that PLACE—alive as you an' me—ain't suppose t'be but they are—full-term an' preemie—hoppin' on like toads out there—mocking everbody that they see—an' then go scoot back to that place—back where that B-Girl went—where all them B-Girls go when they get sick if y'ask me—I know that's where they go—out in that place they got all fenced in like a zoo!

"They're all like this, Mr. Cutter—I got five—no, six of 'em since midnight—they're all—"

An my husband knows all about that bidness too—he hunts an' he fishes out there—yes sir he does—an' he seen her with his own eyes—that girl—that one girl 'specially—

"Ma'am—will you just give us your—"

That black-haired thing they used to have up on that big sign? That one that looked like a witch from the pits a hell? You know her—sign ain't been gone a week—an' you know y'self they don't never take down no sign for no healthy girls—you know that—

"Ma'am—can you just give us your name? Ma'am—your name?"

You just tell th'gummit we know they hidin' somethin' out there—ain't tellin' us all they know—I watch all them medical shows—you tell th'gummit we're onto 'em this time!"

"Ma'am? Lissen now—lissen—"

But the line hummed dead and Mr. Cutter stood up straight, unplugged, and rubbed the place his belly peeped out from the regulation shirt. Buster noticed that the hair was white and thick and whirled there like the splotches on his face, the naval popped up through it lonely like a mushroom left behind in tall grass. The whole thing made Buster sick and he began to stare out toward the exit doors. Some drivers had begun to gather there, in regulation jumpsuits red and new and sparkling silver on the shoulders and the sleeves. It was past time for the second run and only four or five true calls had made it through, the little motels and a few that Medix didn't want, but nothing out-of-state and mostly just wrong numbers lighting up the board. Mr. Cutter cleared his throat and tried to tuck the mushroom and the grass back out of sight.

"Just put her down as a Jane Doe-65. That's how old she said she was, right?"

"Yes sir."

"Good. Well—do it now. Right there after the time. And Welborne," he tugged at his belt and the pickle smell came stronger than before, "I don't care if they think they got the Triple-X Motel—adlib that greeting one more time and you're out of here. You got that?"

"Yes Sir."

And Cutter brushed on by, his pickle smell and belly hair and mushroom naval moving in a stop and go on down the line, behind the other boys all working hard to look awake and eager on the phones. Buster watched the blinking lights and glanced with envy at the drivers by the doors and tried to bring the proper words to mind.

-2-

The first sign seemed to pop up from the clay not far from where the Kiddie Kuntry road turned east, not far from where it met the Freedom Highway on its straight shot from the Strip. Both sides were lettered just the same, a sweeping scrawl of black that dripped in places like a fresh-made cut, in jagged streaks that globbed along the bottom drying hard and glinting sometimes when the sun hit right.

B E W A r E

M O N s T e R s

And then a week went by, the letters fading in the sun and two light storms that drizzled down a cold rain whipped and tumbled and gone stinging in the wind. B E W A r E was still there clear but M O N s T e R s nearly lost when two more jumped up by a stand of pines, their faces whiter, bigger too and letters thicker on the white, the two now further down the Kiddie Kuntry road and pointed toward the gate. The first:

DANGER

MONSTERS

And the second:

HEALTH

HAZARD

AHEAD

Halloween had brought a bumper crop, big and small and one a banner in the trees, a fat and pointed head close toward the center with its eyes and mouth and nose all drawn in wrong and twisted to the side: MONSTERS SUCK. And the others seemed to push up jagged from the brush, out from palmetto thickets and among the cedars, pine and oak as if the birds had dropped some strange and fertile seed to root and bud and blossom in a day. The most of them were painted yellow and their letters red and bold, skulls and crossbones down below fluorescent green and glowing in the dark, clustered in a snake-like reaching from the woods. And soon the signs were everywhere along the road, in bunches there impaled on sticks and poles and branches of the trees, down toward the gate a half a mile of curve and dip and double-back to cross a little stream, the signs poked up on both sides now, two coming back for every one torn down, a silent waiting thick and with a clack like bones in every wind that blew.

DANGER BEWARE DANGER MONSTERS BEWARE

WARNING MONSTERS WARNING HEALTH DANGER WARNING

DANGER HEALTH WARNING MONSTERSMONSTERSMONSTERS MONSTERS

DANGERDANGERDANGER BEWARE BEWAREBEWAREBEWARE

WARNING MONSTERS MONSTERS MONSTERS BEWARE HEALTHWARNING

And in the week before Thanksgiving Day, the leaflets fell each afternoon, like giant yellow snowflakes in a puff and drop and flutter out behind the little planes come low and quick across the swamp, with dollar bills green-sprinkled through the yellow in a dumping straight above the Kiddie Kuntry grounds and then another out along the Strip and back for one last flurry on the town:

M O N S T E R S M U S T D I E

-3-

Lawyer Shadwell smiled at Mr. Cibber and then poured himself another brandy, just enough this time and swirling smooth and fragrant in the snifter, round and round a slow and easy slide that made him sigh and lean against the padded bar. The top floor penthouse at the Triple-X Motel was dimly lit, the drapes still open and the evening sun a pinkish glow across the western sky. Mr. Shadwell sighed again and sipped his brandy. Mr. Cibber sat down on a nearby stool and watched the evening sun go finally down. He sounded tired.

"Simply beautiful. Like Natchez-nouveau columns with a swirl of fluted Mobile-marbling at the base."

"What's that you say?"

"The sky is beautiful."

"It is indeed. Yes."

Mr. Shadwell put the snifter down and turned full toward the window, arms and elbows resting on the bar and his broad back pressing deep into the padding. The sky had turned a color close to purple where the tallest clouds had gathered to the north. Mr. Cibber coughed and rubbed a finger gently back and forth across his nose. And then he got the business rolling once again.

"A fine job of presentation, Thomas. Excellent saturation. The airplanes especially. A very nice touch. Nostalgic. Word War Two vintage, correct?"

"Yes. Reproductions. But detail-perfect all the same. Our Japanese division. On loan from Sporus West."

"Hawaii?"

"Yes. Homma Brothers, Inc. The youngest brother, I believe. Masaharu."

"Ah—him. I remember him well. We worked together once. Years ago. He's very good. Very—thorough."

"He was first choice. Division East is certainly big on him. So I went along."

"Will there be more events?"

"Perhaps. They sent us quite a prospectus. A real wish-book of options. Ways of proceeding. And Sledge hasn't responded. So it may take a bit more preparation. Only time will tell."

"There isn't much of that left, Thomas, I'm afraid. They've decided on an Aztec theme. Did you know?"

"Aztec?"

"Yes. I was wrong about the Egyptian. And the Sumerian-Revival as well. Did you deal with Masaharu personally?"

"No—not directly. With a Mr. Iwabuchi."

"Ah yes. Iwabuchi. Sanji Iwabuchi. The Hommas' good right arm. The Shark. He's blunt as you no doubt discovered. But most effective. He can work wonders. He fixed that leper colony problem worldwide in about a week. Acreage acquisition in the millions."

"He did that?"

"Yes. Division sent you to the right people."

"I've no complaints. Aztec, you say?"

"The final word. I'm not altogether pleased. Too many feathers for my taste. Too squat and gaudy. But—I can make it work. Even here."

The sky was dark beyond the windows now, the room reflected in the glass a framed and hazy stretch of tiny lights across the two men at the bar, bulged larger than they really were and seeming to be floating in the air. And then a blast of red went up outside, a single shaft that burned in through the fuzzy picture-room, off distant in a flash that lit the clouds like lightning out before a storm. Then two more sprang up on each side and more and more until the dark was boiling red out where the sun had gone. Mr. Shadwell rolled a sip of brandy on his tongue and let it go down slow. He hoped the business would be finished soon. The red outside was dropping to a glow with dark smoke up above and rising in a curl and dip that looked like fingers scratching at the sky.

"Not much visual improvement, Cibber—not much at all. Full Carnal Service is a major draw I know, but—whenever it includes that part as well it tends to—to overpower—no matter what you try to do. Even limited-access-burning leaves that—that smell for days. And the ash. And that red—the color—ugh."

"Yes. But the new facilities are cleaner at least."

"Oh? Federal Health Department Order finally came, did it?"

"Yes. And the ash and odor problems are solved. That new Ohlendorf EG-II filter system is ninety-eight percent effective—barely a trace gets through. And then there's the magnolia."

"Beg pardon?"

"We opted for magnolia. Finally. The scent. And it is close to that. To magnolia."

"Magnolia. And Medix paid the installation?"

"Yes. And I must admit that I'm very grateful. It was much more than a nuisance. The problem. It was very serious. Right from the first. You know the standing order as well as I do. Carnal Disposal Centers rarely receive affirmative response from Regional. In most cases they are summarily dismissed as unsuitable for resort development. But this site is perfect and since Medix was already here, we were permitted to compromise—to reach a decent agreement with them. Before their new facilities officially opened. I'm rather proud of the way things worked out."

"I expect you are, Calvin, yes indeed. A remarkable blitz."

"Thank you, Thomas. I'm relieved it went as smoothly as it did. I'm thankful for that. And the new Medix facilities even fit in nicely with the Aztec theme—"

"They do?"

"Almost perfectly. As a backdrop. The second stage. For my Sun Temple and Royal Gardens."

"I see. Well then. That about does it. Yes?"

"All but Sledge."

"Yes yes—Mr. Sledge. A definite problem, to be sure. But not for long. Not for long."

"I hope so, Thomas."

"No—it won't be long now. Everything will come together soon. We'll make our deadline—rest assured of it, Calvin. I'm very near to solving Sledge. Even if the preparations fail. Even then."

"Preparations can be tricky, Thomas. The spin-off. The unforeseen arousal. A very tricky process."

"Yes. Yes I know. But there are other pressures one can use. Many others. My man at the State Bureau says there's no record of inspection. Absolutely nothing. Did you know that?"

"Why no—you mean they—"

"Right—no one checked. No one came to see. So he just kept going, I suppose. On his own. And now—well, you saw what he's got going—you saw that mess out there—"

Mr. Cibber watched the glow and rolling smoke and pushed a button on the bar to bring the drapes a slide and hum and click together in the sudden quiet of the room.

-4-

The picketers had been few at first, five or six old men and several women dressed in coats a size too big, a part-time only line of walking scarecrows someone drove down to the Kiddie Kuntry gate. Their signs were hand-painted and their faces red and twitching when they shouted at a passing car or truck. It didn't seem like much at all at first, the traffic never heavy and the people on the inside seldom seen and nothing moving but the picketers in a shuffle-step and talking to themselves most hours of the day.

But the television crew had come to see the fuss, the field reporter tall and tanned and marching with the scarecrows for a little way, and in a day or two the others had arrived. The signs grew bigger and the picketers too, the men and women young and strong enough to march all day, their campfires spreading out on both sides of the road by night, a blinking in the woods and smoke that drifted thick and lazy toward the swamp. But no one did a thing inside the gate, an old man sometimes sitting there at night and women in the daytime stepping off the hours in a kind of walking prayer, a mumbling mostly lost among the noise the picketers made.

The County Health Department trucks had raised a rolling cloud of dust behind them on the road, at dawn with sunshine streaking just the treetops and the campfires nearly gone. And Sheriff's vans had come in too with dogs to push the picketers on back toward the Strip. One big woman, dressed up like a nurse, let the first truck roll in through the gate but kept the rest outside, an hour almost in among the dust and watching close until the truck had made it out again. And then the county men hung the orange signs all down the fence and on the gate, a hundred yards along the road with yellow rope strung stake to stake and yellow pennants flapping in a sea-breeze come up filled with stinging rain.

xxxxQUARANTINExxxx

The campfires now were closer to the glowing red above the chimneys near the swamp, their smoke together sometimes when the wind blew right and sweetness in the air at night, a flower smell down in a winter chill and taste of salt that came in thick and bitter with the dawn.

-5-

Congee heard the laughter plain, the Dial-A-Borts up there above, up on the clean cement again all neat and dressed in red. And wearing gloves, white gloves that never had to soak for hours in a tub, that never touched a thing but polished gears and turning-clamps and shiny nozzles on a hose. Congee dug a shovel in the trough and scraped along the bottom where a sticker might be caught down in the slush and thickened foam. The ovens back behind were hissing like a snake tonight, the roller-troughs much fuller now and sometimes catching just before he pushed their noses in an open door and bucked them up one good hard kick to let the soup slide deep inside. Congee was a Sticker-Sweep, a Medix SSW Second-Class. He worked the troughs to keep them flowing free and rolling click-click back and forth and back and forth from where the Dial-A-Borts flushed out their vans.

The loads had come in four an hour since the shift began, the hoses nearly off the ground, packed tight and squeaking as they flushed and little time to rest. Black Johnny was the closest Sweep, the only one still there from when they first took Congee on, two months ago and back before the changes came, the four-night shifts and no more masks and the flower smell and vans from places far away now flushing up above. Black Johnny told him just last night he'd seen two New York Dial-A-Borts and one from Bangor, Maine.

"They rollin' from all over. Boss Fuller say we got us a contrack fo' all them states up nawth. All comin' here. Big money, Congee. Big money now!"

Congee caught a Sticker in along the bottom corner, not yet hard but close enough to make the soup splash on his chest and arms each time the blade pushed down. The soup smelled sweet and sometimes made him think of cherry pie and how the Deli Kitchen got on baking day, on Sundays in the Triple-X Motel. He'd worked there for a year and just a few days more. Washing dishes and mopping floors and taking out the trash. But the money wasn't near as good as here. And Christmas Day was half a shift, tomorrow, and a chance to buy some pie and eat it at a shiny table at the Mall.

PART TWO

"The Girl From Tennessee"

CHAPTER SEVEN

Judy liked the Big Boys' Chorus best of all, four rows beside the manger scene and voices strong and loud enough to reach the little Hoppers out along the walls, to make it to the places where they hid among the tinsel and the pine-rope thick as carpet or an old-time curtain pulled across a cluttered stage. The Recreation Hall was brightly lit, in blinking colors high up where the children couldn't reach, the windows framed in steady greens and reds and doors a jumble of gold to blue with something like a ball of mistletoe above each one. The Big Boys made the children jump around and try to sing.

Gooo tellit anna muntin
Ooooveh hells anna fah a-wah
Gooo tellit anna muntin

She didn't look away this time, not even when the Torsos rolled in on their carts, not even when the Fun-Heads danced in hard with mouths like wounds that sucked the air and eyes bulged out so far they seemed about to pop. Not even when the ones came riding in that the nurses hid away most times until the others had been bathed and fed. The ones they carried in their arms or down in sacks upon their backs. The ones she'd never seen up close before. She didn't look away.

Ooooveh hells anna fah a-wah

Parker waved from over by the tree, the presents stuffed in there around it in a jagged circle glittered from the paper and the bows, the silver sparkling brightest but the gold a deeper almost-glow that caught the big lights as they flickered on. And Parker stuffed in more, two boxes and a flutter-down of tiny bags with ribbon-ties and everything looked new and clean and fresh just like it had back years ago before she started in to run. The Big Boys never seemed to stop for air.

Gooo tellit anna muntin

And all the children that could do it clapped and jumped and gave the grownups fits to keep them off the tables filled with food. And smells like years ago, of ham and turkey, sweet potato pie and chocolate cake and bowls and bowls of pudding light and dark and apples red and speckled, big and little for the mouths that sang and sang and chanted long and loud each time the Birthday Baby's name came round again.

Tee-thus K-ryst e bone!

Tee-thus Tee-thus Tee-thus

She sat down in a shadow over near the tumbling-mats, beside a brightly colored stack that reached above her head and pushed back almost flush against the wall. Pine boughs were packed in tight and thick along its sides with two fat branches on the top turned upward like a wind had come in strong from where the children played. She felt much better now, the daily sickness all but gone away in bites of cracker that the big nurse made her take, and Parker like he always was, a gentle prod and leading into naptime and a slow walk through the growing darkness arm-in-arm. And nothing had seemed better until now, the quiet then around them soft and every crunching sound their shoes had made dropped quick and lost below them one by one. But when the children came to sing among the pine and colors of the Hall all thick and mingled with the good smells everywhere, she felt a thing inside her deep and warm begin to open in the places only Parker knew were there. He walked her through the dance a little while and then he made her step aside and found a chair and went alone to help the Big Boys line up for their song. The Hoppers had begun to jump around, out further from the wall with nearly every up-and-down, a boy-girl there the strongest and their hair a blur of golden in the light.

Gooo tellit anna muntin

Jump around and jump-around, it looked like fun from where she sat. Jump jump and skip and hop and never take too long to rest. Jump-around like Hoppers free and further from the wall, out closer to the children's dance, the Big Boys trying hard to start another song. It looked like fun.

Sah-lint nye
Oh—oh-lee nye

And jump-around had been her own life near at hand, not way back in the running days but down in Strips along the southern coast and west one time to Kansas for a year. A jump-around and moving all the time. But nothing like the children now, not anything like that. Her own a jump and go without a rest or ending ever there.

Ah e kahm
Ah e bride

The Silver Beaver-jump the worst of all the others first to last, her legs not strong like what had got her down the mountain and away, the jumps-and-goes sometimes too high and fast for anything but pills to keep her on the pace. And Copper just the last one in a line that pushed back night by night to where it all began, the running first and faces closing in, and faces like those first ones every step along the way, beyond the lights and deep in smoke a grinning in and out. She didn't want to think about the running now, the Big Boys and the children now there to help her mind stay free, like Copper and the other Coppers near and far who brought the chicken-wire across her stage.

Slee-pee hebben-eee peas
Slee-e-pee hebben-eee peas

But nothing in that jump and go and jump-around had done the things that Parker did, had touched her in the way his fingers rubbed a slow and warming while to help her sleep. Or taught her how to love the baby down inside and laugh to feel it sometimes kick and bump and flutter up against him when the bad dreams brought her back awake. When he lay down beside her close and held her then until the dreams were gone. The Hoppers bumped the boy-girl free and off into a little whirl of up-and-down and slide to miss the others on the floor. They seemed to really see her now. The boy waved first and then the girl, their heads together cheek to cheek and both mouths opened wide.

Sah-lint nye
Oh-oh—lee nye

And nothing more than touch and hold and warm, a month or more past when he asked, out on the swamp in fog all deep and something dead and rotting near at hand, a smell that made her want to leave, a dead smell mixed with sweet and water in a slap and suck against his boat all soft and steady and a crying bird above them in the sky. He took her there to fish. He spoke first.

"I—look, I think—I—I know—yes—I know it now—"

"Know what?"

She still could see him there, his blond hair bristly on the sides and skin just like the leather of her favorite purse. His face was long and nose a little twisted to the side and eyes that made her think of mountain sky, a blue so deep and clear it almost hurt to look for long, pressed in the red-flecked wrinkles of his skin like pools of crystal water sprung up whole in desert land. He shifted in the boat and made the slap and suck grow louder than before.

"I need someone—I—I need—"

It took a long time to say, the slap and suck gone quiet by the time he made the words come out, the bird cry fading off and just a whine of something like a chainsaw at the very last.

"I want—I—I want you to marry me. Can you do that?"

But then the other boat had whined in fast and pushed by in a spray of green that rocked their boat and took her fishing pole away. The other voice had seemed to be beside her in the falling green, come in a shriek but gone as soon as Parker touched her hand.

Look out—too close—they seen us—too close goddammit!

The boy-girl had begun a bowing jerk and twist that made her think of how the ac/dcs danced, the late show crowd that sometimes stayed past closing time. They even tried to rip away the chicken-wire her first night there. But Copper called the B-Boys in and cleared the room.

Ah e kahm
Ah e bride

The other boat had turned around, a whine and whump-whump groan down further in the fog, the voice come shrieking out again but this time in a way that made her think of Copper and that last night at the club. When he had told he what she had to do.

"Don't give me nothin' but a yes, bitch! Don't give me nothin' I don't want a hear!"

"But—but I just—"

"Don't say it now! You goddammit you just don't say nothin' but yes—say it!"

"I—I just can't—"

And whump-whump turned full into whine again and Parker had got them moving fast as he could go, the voices close at first then far away like Copper when he came to find her in the woods. Her face had hurt a little bit, a stinging gone away the more she ran, just pointing where she thought the north might be, toward nowhere special but some lights off distant in the night. And then the boat had picked up speed, rain in the wind and biting at her face, a sting and throb but not like Copper's hand and Parker there this time to lead her home. But first they hid beneath a bluff and listened while the shriek and whine died off to nothing and a thumping boom like thunder came to take its place.

"Maybe—maybe they're duck hunters. I run into them once in awhile. Not so many ducks around here anymore. Or fish. I guess I haven't caught a fish in over five years. And even then I threw it back. It looked funny to me. There used to be a lot of ducks though. Even when the fish began to play out. Every year. Migrating ducks. And hunters. Hunting clubs."

"But why did they do that? Chase us like that?"

"Hard to tell. Could be Medix men. They carry guns too. And Medix owns most of Sutter's Swamp. What's left of it. They sometimes forget they don't own it all."

"Who owns the rest?"

"I do. Here and back where they found us. They police it sometimes. To stop BD's—to stop the dumping."

"BDs?"

"Bulk-Disposal—by the independents. When there's an overflow. Not many of them left down here though. A few, I guess. Medix changed things. New ways of doing things. Now it's mostly special ovens. And liquid—liquidi-fication—I think that's the word. Nobody knows where all of it goes. But the Swamp is getting smaller. All but my piece."

"Here? They—they dump the—"

"I think so. Yes—the bulk-ash. And the other thing. The liquid thing. I do know we don't find near as many babies now. Since Medix came."

The boy-girl had begun to rock and sway, alone and separate from the singing and the dance, the other Hoppers bumping back now to a jumping distance from the wall. The boy was smiling and the girl had pulled her hair down nearly to her nose.

And jump around and jump-around and Silver Beaver gone for good and all she knew and deep down sure and in her growing like the baby Parker helped her keep, the jump-around all ended on the truck ride back to where the children lived, to where the special ovens didn't reach.

"Like I said—I want you to marry me. Will you do it?"

"It's—I—I ain't had much luck at—"

"I know it's quick. I know that. But I know it's right."

"Is—is it the baby? Is that why you—"

"The baby needs a daddy. They all do."

"Like them kids you a'ready got? Like them?"

"What?"

"You their daddy too?"

And he had looked surprised, like somehow it had never come to him before, the children reaching out for him, the ones with arms and hands, but all the rest gone at him in whatever way they could, to feel his touch down on their heads or holding warm and steady when they cried. It seemed it never came to him before.

"And me, Parker?"

"You?"

"After the baby comes. What then?"

"We'll find a good name. A really good name."

"And me?"

He had reached to touch her, fingers closing on her shoulder in a tug and pull that brought her close beside him in what seemed more dream than real. The jump-around began to bump away down underneath the truck tires on the rutted road, a bumping down and lost for good and gone and she had felt the tears upon her cheeks so hot, the taste a strong one salty on her lips and dying quickly, wiped away like Copper's voice and stinging hand, the smoke and faces in the dark and fingers reaching for her through the chicken-wire. All gone beneath his touch, the truck stopped just outside the gate, his eyes turned wider than the sky when he moved in to kiss her on the cheeks and lips and forehead then, a blue come down to catch and hold and wash her clean again.

"I love you."

"I—I love you too, Parker. I do—but—but I—"

"What?"

"I've done things. Way back and recent too. Too many things. This baby—it comes of all the things I—"

"Will you marry me or won't you? It's almost EveningSing and I need to find my donkey hat. Well?"

"Yes."

The word had come out slow, within a long breath and her head down on his shoulder then, pressing up against the rough cloth of his shirt all muffled and alone. And he had kissed her lips again and went to open up the gate.

CHAPTER EIGHT

Parker and the Big Boys were together now, arms linked and swaying back and forth just like the little Hoppers near the wall, the boy-girl all alone and jumping to the place she sat, a few feet distant and their free arm flapping like a bird about to fly. Judy smiled and clapped her hands and held one out a roosting place in case they chose to land and stay. And the singing started in again and louder than before and Parker there the loudest of them all. It seemed like years since they had sat outside the gate, the things that rose up since all dark and fearful, fire upon the sky at night and voices taunting from the woods. At first he said the wedding would be soon, two weeks away or maybe three, and then when he could find a preacher brave enough to come. They talked about it just last night.

"We don't have to do that, Parker. Not now. Not with everything that's going on. Why can't we just say the words ourselves? There's Bibles here. I seen 'em."

"No—that's not the way. It's got to be done right. I want it done right."

"It's all for them, ain't it? The nurse. Them nuns. I know they a'ready don't like me—blame me for what's happening. Is it—"

"No. It's for us. And they like you fine."

But they had never made her feel at home, a little frown sometimes or shaking of their heads when they had thought she couldn't see. The quarantine had made it worse, the monster signs and marching people on the road, their angry shouts not hitting Big Nurse half so hard as when the county trucks came in to try and take the children back to town. And it was Big Nurse who had met them at the gate and only one tall skinny man had gotten inside long enough to meet with Parker by the office door. The man had opened up a metal-covered book and read awhile before he finally spoke.

"Are you Mr. Parker Sledge?"

"I am."

"How many confirmed cases are there?"

"Cases? Cases of what?"

"Complaint Order says ADU—Associational Disease Unspecified—B-Girl Probable and Public Disposal Fugitive, I-A."

"None."

"Beg pardon?"

"There are no cases of anything here."

"But—but my orders explicitly state that—"

"There are no sick people here."

"You—you do keep defectives, don't you, Mr. Sledge?"

"Children. This is a Home. A licensed Home."

"Ah yes—but an uninspected Home. You were grandfathered in. I know the record. No inspections. Nothing in the record. But now we've had complaints. Official complaints. Do you harbor Public Disposal Fugitives here?"

"This is a Home."

And all the grownups gathered by the office door, everyone but Big Nurse still out by the gate and Parker's special friend, the old man, Emment gone to give her help. The county man had seemed surprised to see so many people come around.

"Look, Mr. Sledge—let's not play games, shall we?

Let's don't waste each other's time. Let's just lay it all out. Ok?"

"I've been doing—"

"These complaints are binding on my office. There are over fifty separate affidavits. Thirty just last week. Duly sworn witnesses. Evidence. Solid evidence that—"

"Evidence? Of what?"

"Of the sickness here. Public Disposal Fugitives. Pictures of them. Infrared surveillance. Eye-witness accounts of sightings. Is there one Judy Grace Taylor on the premises?"

"Yes. My fiancé."

She had watched their eyes, the nuns and others, even Doc Melrooney on the steps, the look like one of shame or fear there deep and spreading as they tried to keep from showing anything at all. But Parker never let a thing show on his face, his eyes not moving from the county man and his hands dug deep inside the pockets of his coat. Several seagulls had come in to float above the Honor Barn and somewhere further off a sound like fireworks crackled in the rising wind. The county man had shut his metal book and turned to go.

"There's a serious problem here, Mr. Sledge. I can smell it."

"You are welcome to take a look around. We have a doctor on staff. There's nobody sick. Not even a bad cold."

"I don't need to look. These complaints say it all. And what they say to me is quarantine."

"Quarantine! I've told you we have no sick people here. I've told you that. I've offered you the chance to inspect—"

"No need no need. You can't concentrate Public Disposal Fugitives. Not under the new laws. Grandfather or no grandfather. And B-Girl change of domicile—especially an unreported change—and to a place of juvenile concentration—gives an override authority. To act directly and swiftly in the public interest. To isolate irregularities until proper resolution can be made. Did you know that, Mr. Sledge?"

"No—but I have been—"

"I know—grandfathered. And let the public servant find the illegal defectives for himself. Let him secure the B-Girl if he can. Oh yes. And then throw in an innocent Children's Home and use the fiancé dodge to top it off. Oh my yes. It's always something like that with you people. Cracks in the system. But I know those cracks, Mr. Sledge. I know what you grandfathers do. Which research facility are you dealing with? Hoess Medical? Wirtz Surgical? TogoLand Transplant? Or maybe it's—"

"What—what are you talking about?"

"And what is the going rate these days, Mr. Sledge? Is it still so much per organ—sick or well? And let the public welfare be damned? So many dollars per pound? I know the cracks. I've seen them all. But this time is different. This time we're filling in a crack. This time we're taking a stand. This right here is a public health matter and I can act. On my own judgment. Public Disposal Fugitives and unreported B-Girl change of domicile. You're quarantined, Mr. Sledge. And you will stay that way until we decide what else to do. Or—" And he had made his eyes go slit-like in a swirl of blowing sand. "We can take it off your hands. Take in the Defectives—the Fugitives—see that they get proper handling—

return the B-Girl to—"

"No!"

"Final answer, Mr. Sledge?"

"Yes."

"Well then. Have it your way—for now."

And he had left, the trucks in dust around them and behind, the wind turned stronger and the seagulls gone away. And the signs were ugly yellow and the night sky had turned redder than before, with black smoke there by day and more and more like twisters forming in a darkened line across the swamp. The helicopters came to bring in food and everything had dropped down into waiting, silent until now, the day-by-day the same for all the children there, but Christmas Eve the first time that the grownups seemed alive.

#

She smiled to see how Parker loved to sing. A flutter in her belly deep and long seemed almost strong enough to hear. A flutter beat and kick that seemed to reach out toward the dance. She smiled to see the boy-girl stretch their wings to take her hand.

Jo-eee toe de woll
De Lard eee comb!

CHAPTER NINE

The trucks came back, the County-Man alone with Parker for what seemed an hour at the gate. And Big Nurse and a nun or two had stood and watched and sometimes frowned toward Judy as she waddle-paced alone and kicked at clods of clay and tried to make her jacket hide the bloated thing she had become. To hide the ugly and the fat. And waddle-pace and kick and belly blocking out her boots and Parker standing in between the trucks and what they'd come to do. The trucks had roared and rumble-popped and pop-pop-popped alone but Parker wouldn't open up the gate. And she had heard the things they said. The County-Man and Parker back and forth along the fence. The trucks had stopped her evening walk, the waddle down the road, down to the gate and back again with Parker close beside her and the cool air feeling good. But this time they had heard a thunder out toward where the twister-smoke curled up to reach the clouds, back toward the burning-place and flower smell so strong it hurt her nose to breathe. And Big Nurse came and two nuns with her at a run and Emment close behind with a shotgun just in time to see the first truck when it popped in sight.

"Doc heard it on the CB, Mr. Sledge—but we thought tomorrow—not today—"

"I'll talk to them. You all keep clear of it."

And he had left her then to waddle-pace and kick and watch and listen, a roll of dust come up the road and rumble-pop and roar and red dust everywhere and gone to rising like the blackness on the swamp.

#

But it was over now, the fireplace bright with pine-knots and a glowing chunk of oak, her fat-and-ugly in the shadows on the bed, in Parker's room and underneath the quilt he made her use. The bulge was like a giant melon in a sack and pressing hard against her breasts to sometimes take her breath away, down there and with a flutter-kick and bump that kept her eyes from closing and her head just resting light and easy on the pillows he had plumped up nice and firm. Just like the pillows for her feet, the nearly only way that she could see her toes. And then the fire was bright and Parker gone to EveningSing and all the trucks had roared away, the old man Emment's shotgun pointed dead to center of the place the trucks had turned around. And she had waddle-paced and kicked and kicked until the last truck pushed into the dust and Parker came back then to help her home. But she had seen it all and heard it too, the wind just right and voices at the gate and fence grown louder with each and every waddle-step she took. The trucks and voices in the dust and in the drifting smoke and glow of red begun to deepen on the evening sky. And somehow roar and rumble-pop and shout and beat for beat among the whirling dust had made her think of how it was there past and gone, there solid in the running-time down from the mountain hard and fast as she could go, a rumble-pop behind of other trucks and voices in a distance she herself had made. Parker's voice had seemed the loudest in the wind, the running-time at first kept back each time he spoke.

"No! Not a single one—not even one!"

The fire was crackling louder now, a pine knot hissing out a flash of sparkles and the oak log crunching deeper in its coals. Her belly looked so ugly as she tried to walk, a wobble to her legs and ankles puffed until they had to slit her boots to make them fit. And she had watched and listened, pace for pace and Big Nurse and the nuns a frown each time she thought to turn their way. The trucks had made her want to scream.

"You can't keep this up, Sledge. You can't do it!"

"I will not give you a single one!"

"We can take—"

"No!"

The shotgun looked too big for Emment's arms, the barrels glinting in the dying sunlight in a slow sweep up from where he stood, training on the County-Man and one quick glimpse of Copper's face down further in the rumbling dust. A jump-back quick and gone away.

"Hey—hey call him off, Sledge—you can't—"

But Parker let the shotgun stay and Emment pumped it hard and raised it higher, pointing at the place the trucks began to turn around. The dust had risen thicker than before and gone up quick like some red curtain out along the fence. But Copper's face was clear among it all, a quick look full into his eyes and twisted mouth and fist a shake toward where she stood. Then dust so thick the trucks were lost to sight a rumble and a pop and someone shouting something in a voice turned choked and raw just like her father's voice had come out on the night she ran away.

#

The other men had been there with him down beside the fire like dogs too tired to hunt. And she had come to try and bring him home, but careful where she stood and called his name, not close enough for any dog to rise up quick and maybe bite. Her Mama had not known about the night-times in the barn or in his truck, one year down in the darkness that he'd always find before he made her moan and cry. Her body had turned different like a dream gone on past waking up, like pictures in the magazines she read, the ladies pushing out their clothes and smiling at the men, the ladies in her dreams all curve and hollow-plump and her one too so quick it seemed a magic thing. Until the night-times came. Her Mama never knew.

"He's most likely over on Pore's Knob. Back yonder in that logging camp. That's where they drink. You go on and tell him that pieded cow a his'n has run off again—you go an' tell him t'come on home—"

And she had gone up slow and easy in the black, the long way in on up the bear trail steep and sometimes slick from where the rock poked through, on up and up through scraggle-pine and briar, near crawling where the rocks got tight and then a shuffle-step or two and out along the ridge and down for just a little ways until the fire came clear. His voice had been the loudest there, a donkey-bray of song and cursing all around it in a whimper-yelp of dogsound, growling deep and hurting her to hear, a stab down in the places he had touched, a hard and pushing in and in and in the one place he had liked the best. A year of darkness wiping clean away the old time when he taught her how to hunt and fish and ride the plow-horse into town. A wipe-away in moans and cries and fear, all gone away like Christmas toys and candy and the doll he'd made, wiped clean and nothing left behind but shame to mark the trail. And shame and fear together pushed down deep, full deep and cold and like the hole she dug alone and in the hollow by the creek. A hole there deep and wide enough to hide the baby she had lost.

But then a hand reached out to catch and hold her hair, yanked down in stinging pain and arms about her neck and waist and just a glimpse of face behind, a grin there and a smell of dog and whiskey and a voice like dry wood crackling in a fire.

"Hey hey looky—looky here what I gone got me, boys—whoa now—whoa—"

They had stumbled through the brush, the grapevine and the briar pulling at her coat and at the dress her Mama made her wear, the long one she had sewed herself from scraps of cloth, a stumble-slide down to the circle of the fire and near to where the dogs began to stretch themselves and sniff the wind. But she had closed her eyes and fought the arms, full bucking toward the last one like some young mule first time leather touched its back.

"Whoa—whew boys—honey lamb—easy now—easy—whoa—hey looky—hey—hey goddamn—looky here, Pete—hey—ain't this yourn—ain't it?"

And then she opened up her eyes again and saw her father's face.

"Yeah—that's her."

"Whew buddies, son—she done growed up sure's hell!"

His face had been all streaked and striped in light and dark from where the flames threw shadows out to dance across the other stretching dogs and up to color everything that moved, his eyes not aiming at her long before he spoke again, words slurred and deep and lost in whiskey from the jug he held up close against his chest. And whiskey smell like stinging rain gone by her face each time the dog-man back behind her barked. Her father's words came slow and mumbled, nearly lost in dog-growl and in crackle from the fire.

"Yeah—she's nice a'right—nice."

"Nice y'say, Pete? Nice?"

"Yeah—she's a good'n—real good—"

"Shit, son—shit, now—"

The other dogs had stood up slow, all looking like the hounds that she could hear in yodel-yelp and whoop up higher in the woods, the dog-men sniffing at the place she bucked and bumped, a grin on every dog-man there, tongues moving slowly over lips and eyes gone wide and shadow-caught all dark and dancing as they came.

"What's y'thinkin' on us maybe givin' her a try, Pete?"

But he had never said a word at first, just swaying there and jug brought up to drink a bit and let down slow again against his chest.

"Pete? Whoa now, honey—hey Pete! Y'got ya a live'n here, son—an' big—whoa—goddamn—she done growed a whole lots now!"

She bucked away the fingers on her breast, pressed down hard and pushing past the buttons Mama sewed, pressed in and pinching at her there, the place that he had licked and sucked at in the darkness and alone. But the other dog-men had come close before the one behind her said another word.

"Pete? Hey—hey you gone deef there, son?"

"Naw—naw I'm hearin' ya."

"Then how's about it, Pete Hey now—hey now dar-lin' whoa—"

And even now, alone and safe and nothing near to make her feel afraid, the fire a happy one and thick quilt there to hide her ugly and her fat, with Parker coming back to hold her close and maybe rub her off to sleep, even here and now she wasn't sure if she had really heard him say the words or if she somehow made them up just when her teeth had found the fingers on a buck and jump and clamped down tearing at the sour-taste until the blood had joined it warm and salty in a shriek of whiskey-smell and pain.

"I ain't carin' which nor whether about it"

The words had seemed to come from him, from where he still stood swaying like a tree about to fall, the words come out almost the second she had chewed up blood and bucked out long enough to roll back from the dog-men closing in. Back to the bear-trail and away, the howling there behind and two shots fired from somewhere going high and tearing through the pine like icy rain above her head.

"I ain't carin' which nor whether"

Down down and rolling sometimes, briar-caught and ripping at her coat and dress, on down on hands and knees and breaking free out where a bald began, and trucks behind a rumble-roar and shouts and dog-whoops long and short, the moon come out and head-lights bobbing up above up where the log road snaked out from the camp. She ran and ran and never let her Mama see her when she got back home, gone straight to find the cardboard suitcase hidden in the barn and money in a glass jar underneath the willow by the creek, the coins and crumpled dollar bills she made from selling honey and the times she got his wallet when the whiskey made him sleep, all ready for the day she'd thought might never come. The ocean calling clear, the far-off ships and waves and sandy beach like pretty pictures in a book. But back in the woods a half-run first with suitcase banging on her hip, down to the trails that only she could find, down down and solid gone from where the headlights bobbed like fireflies floating through the trees.

"I ain't carin' which nor whether"

CHAPTER TEN

She tried to make her toes touch underneath the quilt but fat and blanket gave her legs a pain, pushed high and shooting in a sting like what had come upon her by the time the trucks had rolled off in the rising dust. When Parker finally came to finish up their walk. His eyes had rings of red around them and his hair looked caked in dust. Big Nurse and the nuns had gone with Emment to the gate, to help him get set up inside the little booth.

"That won't do much good, I guess. One shotgun won't stop much of anything. If they go outside the law."

Parker's voice had sounded tired, the walk a short one and the sun dropped down below the treetops when they turned in at his door. And she had held his arms and tried to make her own voice come out brave.

"But not now. Not today. They won't do anything today."

"No. Not today."

"They're gone, Parker."

"Yes. For now. I don't think they'll sneak back in. I suspect they're afraid of catching something."

And he had helped her settle in, to take a nap before he brought some food. The hat he wore for EveningSing had made her laugh.

"That—that thing looks like a bird—a big-eyed bird—like an owl—"

"It is—a bird. But it's supposed to be an eagle."

"Eagle? Oh no—no—that doesn't look like no eagle—not with them eyes—it's an owl."

"It's supposed to be an eagle. See the beak? And

the wings? Owls don't have wings like this—wings shaped like this—"

He had fluffed and poked and made its head bounce up and down, the wings curved sharp behind it almost touching at the tips. The beak looked set to bite his nose and both eyes were pushed back into the feathers deep and almost gone away. She had laughed again and stretched out underneath the quilt. The fat-and-ugly there but calmer, hidden and at rest between the flutter-kicks and bumping rolls and stabs of pain. He stirred the fire and stood back up. The bird had slipped a wing down almost past his ear. And he had a little trouble buttoning up his coat.

"You rest. Then we'll eat and maybe talk some more."

"About the County-Men? About what they—"

"It's getting late. I've got to—"

"But you stopped 'em, Parker. They can't come in here if you don't let 'em. They can't do that, can they?"

"You rest now."

"I saw Copper there, Parker. I think I saw him. In one of them trucks."

"There were a lot of men in the trucks. From different places. Different agencies."

"To take the children?"

"We'll talk later."

"No—no I want to know. Now. Not later—now. Is it only the children?"

"Mostly yes. The most severe cases—I think that's what he said—the most severe cases. It's still unsettled."

"Unsettled? But—"

"Their papers weren't in order. They need another judge—another court to make it solid. I've read the new laws. They need more than they've got."

"But—but the last time that County-Man acted like he could—"

"He was wrong. It takes more. If they go at it legally it takes more. They haven't even inspected—they don't have recent figures—numbers, how many children are here. Dates. Ages. Names. Color-codes—the new Race Classification Law says they need to specify the primary 'color' of each child. They need all that before they can remove anybody. And our license doesn't mention inspection at all. So—it's optional for us. We don't have to let them in. Legally. Unless two judges say to do it, we don't have to do a thing ourselves. Nothing. And even then—all they can do is inspect—the first time is only for inspection. An official one. To catalogue. And that buys us some time. To figure out what's best to do. But look—we can talk later—you need to rest."

"And me?"

"What?"

"They still want me, don't they? That—that's why Copper was—"

"You're my fiancé. I've even filed the papers."

"But—"

"Just rest. The point is that everything is still unsettled. Unresolved. They acted too quickly. Got ahead of themselves. Ahead of the law. Like that quarantine. It's a stand-off. Legally it's not binding. But I doubt they'll lift it anyway. Not after they've gone this far. Not now. Not with the TV coverage and all the rest of it. We've been on the news a good bit here of late. And too many people're thinking we're all dying of some disease—that we're fixing to send out germs to kill them in their beds."

"What about food—the helicopters they've—"

"That will probably stop. Soon. But we're ok. For awhile at least. We've been stockpiling. And there are other ways to bring in more. Enough to give us breathing time I think."

"But why are they doing all this? Why are they—"

"Something's stirred things up. Put a spotlight on us. Medix. That county agent thinks we're selling diseased organs. Maybe it's Medix. Or maybe it's the Sporus men. Most likely it's Sporus."

"Them two men that came out here?"

"Yes. They want my land."

"But what are we going to do? What can we—"

"We're getting married next week. Did I tell you I finally found a preacher?"

"You did? But when did—"

"This morning. Doc made contact. On the radio. Our private network. He's Pentecostal. The preacher. Do you mind?"

"What?"

"That he's Pentecostal. The preacher Doc found? I didn't know how that would—"

"And he'll come here?"

"Yes. He's from Slackbridge. That's up north a bit. Near Macon, I think. Somewhere. Billy Manatee. That's his name. He'll be here next Saturday."

"Next Saturday?"

"Yes. And you don't mind?"

"Mind?"

"Like I said—he's Pentecostal—and some people

don't like—"

"No—that's fine—I don't know much about all that stuff anyways. You—you're sure he'll come here?"

"Yes. Doc said he sounded pretty normal—they sometimes get real loud, y'know. The few I've known did. But," and he had smiled and fluffed the wing up off his ear, "so do we."

He had kissed her as he left, the bird a flop and flap of feathers from behind, wide-bottomed like a setting hen and wings swept up and out and nearly catching on the door when he passed through. And she had dozed and woke up once or twice with Copper's face almost alive and dancing in the fireplace light. But Copper was the last one clear among the running and the fear, down from the mountain just fifteen and keeping to the places where the moon could not get in, in shadows on a trail nobody else would even think to use, the trucks behind and lights a jog and dance above then gone out one by one. But it had sometimes seemed the trucks had never gone away at all, behind her down the years of running state to state, the first town like the next and every one together now a blur of smoke and grinning faces in the little rooms, each place just like the one she'd left to run some more. And voices too, the men like what she'd run from all gone whooping in the smoke and whiskey-smell. And hands come up like bird-claws in a scratch and pull to shake the chicken-wire or dropped down slow upon their laps, beneath the newspapers or the magazines a rub and rustle with the music and the losing of her costume piece by piece. She met the first tall Copper in a place called Martinsville, the bus gone on without her and her money nearly spent. She hadn't had enough to make it even halfway to the coast.

“But you don’t need no money t’get there, darlin’. Not you.”

She smoothed the quilt down on her chest, the cloth a crinkle in among the fireplace sounds, the pain not half so bad and running years too blurred to hold to or to bring in clear enough to see. Not staying long enough to study out but beatings turned to bump and turned to jump-around and Copper-faces bouncing with the rush and flow of smoke and whoops and voices pushed out through the night. And hatred for her Daddy there and strong inside of every Copper that she saw, deep down in every fist or flat-hand on her face and every rider’s push in hard and hot and there with power in her body going out to make the grinning faces howl and moan but never touch her when she danced.

You tease ‘em, see? Just give a peek at first. Like this—yeah—and drop a little there—just side to side and shake a little just a little just a little

Yeah—and lord god girl go—bump yeah bump yeah bump bump yeah—go—yeah—yes yes yes

Oh yes—like this—like—what—I—like I—like—I—showed—you

Oh god mama—shit—oh god—mamamamamama—c’mere mama—oh god c’mere

The fireplace popped and crackled louder now, the fire blazed up and smell of pine and something else there too, and other voices, maybe just the one, a little voice like music or a stream of cold air rippling through it all from first down to the last, from when she buried what had come out hot and fearful back up on the mountain in the night, on through the others three or more, the babies lost before she felt a thing, the doctor-tended one, the Medix one there strongest in her now, the voice raised up to dance down in the pop and crackle, in the hiss and rising sputter of the fire. A sound like bees, like humming bees was there.

Mmmmmmmmmmmmmmmmmmmmmmmmmm

Then gone, dropped off and sucked quick into hiss and pop again, lost for awhile in smoke and curl of flame all jagged-licking at the log. With just a whisper-echo left like what was there from Parker when she told him everything there was to tell.

That doesn't matter anymore

It's over

Finished

And I don't care about it now

I don't care

She felt the flutter-kick and bump and tried to move her legs apart, the quilt so heavy now and warm beyond a comfort on her chest, the Copper-faces turned to smoke a bobbing mix of light and dark and Parker feathered like an owl come down to gently sweep the air.

CHAPTER ELEVEN

Judy watched the preacher's wife and how she made the children laugh and jump and dance around, the Hoppers and the Boy-Girl in a funny clog-step side-to-side each time the fiddle reached up high. The preacher's wife had fiddled for an hour now, the Hoppers holding back at first until she found their hiding place and led them with her to the stage. The fiddle sounded sweet, a sad soft tune that Judy knew from somewhere far away and gone, at preaching in the springtime and a dinner-on-the-grounds. Her mother there and other ladies too, her father off somewhere and drinking with the men, herself too little and too young for notice to be taken, nothing special but her eyes the grannies said were sure to break a heart some day. The tune had been there strong among the honeysuckle smell and in the speckled light upon the tables and the quilts, the fiddler tall that day and old-time whiskered, beard all long and white just like the Bible-men inside her mother's heavy book, like Moses with that rod stuck out and beating on the sea. And he had played and played and sometimes sang a little bit, a verse or two with fiddle resting up against his chest and bow flung out and tapping at the air. Just like the preacher's wife did now, the Hoppers trying hard to help, their little arms above their heads and flapping sometimes to the beat she gave.

God give No-e the rainbow sign
don't you see,
God give No-e the rainbow sign
don't you see,

The Big Boys made a thunder-sound, their boots a stomp and kick hard on the wooden floor beside the stage, their voices mixing sometimes with the Hopper-flap and high clear notes the preacher's wife laid down. The song was nearly done.

God give No-e the rainbow sign
    no more water but a fire next time
no mah wah-tah no mah no mah

Judy sat alone, the chairs pushed back and no one at the table now but her, the supper done and Parker and the preacher gone to help the Torsos and the Fun-Heads into bed, the rest gone too all but the Hoppers and the Big Boys as the preacher's wife began another tune.

Light's in the val-ley—out-shine the sun

Doc and Emment were the first to leave, to walk the fence and put out fires, the little ones the torches and the burning arrows made, streaked in all week it seemed as soon as sundown came. And people out there yelling in the dark each time one hit.

Light's in the val-ley—out-shine the sun

All week the campfires toward the swamp had spread out brighter, mixing in a flash and curl against the red glow in the sky, more and more of them and bigger warning signs by day, poked up above the scrub and little pines and County-Men and Sheriffs there too, just past the fence and sometimes pushing back the people come in close to watch and yell.

Light's in the val-ley—out-shine the sun

Parker never let on what he felt, just smiling mostly even when a big fire blazed up quick. But she had noticed how the others jumped and she had seen the packing going on, the extra food in boxes and the bags of clothes and children's toys. And sometimes it was nearly dawn before he got free long enough to check on how she was.

Look a-way be-yond the blue

Big Nurse and a nun were sweeping in the place the rice got spilled, across the room where Preacher Manatee had stood. The wedding had been loud.

I took Jesus as my savior,
    You take Him too,

Judy brushed away a line of crumbs, almost hidden up beneath the lacework on her sleeve. The gown was homemade; an older nun had sewed it into shape last night back in the women's dorm. Judy had stood on a crate and Big Nurse and the other women watched. The lace was old, a yellow touch there in it taking off the white. The nun had smiled a lot, like Big Nurse and the rest, all smiles and giggles sometimes too, their faces keeping nothing of the way they used to look when she came near. It took a long long time to fix the dress.

I took Jesus as my savior,
    You take Him too—hallelujah

The nun had pricked her finger once, the needle drawing just a little blood but not a drop got on the cloth. The women had brought in tea and cake and Big Nurse had a pint of something she called joy.

"Now I don't usually encourage this sort of thing—but—"

"But?"

"But for special times—well—"

"What is it?"

"It's joy, honey. Pure bottled joy."

"What is it really?"

"Take a taste—just a sip now—here use these little cups—just a taste. You too, Judy—it won't hurt what's working there inside you—not a bit—there you go—drink up."

"It—it's real good. It's a wine—"

"No—no it's not. It's different—not a wine. What is it? What do you think it is?"

But Judy hadn't said a thing and drank two cups and then the preacher's wife came in and Big Nurse hid the bottle in behind a fern.

I took Jesus as my savior,

You take Him too,

The joy had tasted hot and nearly sour, biting at her tongue and catching in her throat but warm and soothing at the last. It made her think (not for very long but there and strong and flashed away) a thought of vodka in her glass and everything gone shiny at the Beaver when her show was almost done. A little thought and sucked off quick but with her while it lasted like a tug of needle through the lace, a pull back to a life that called again and made her sad.

Look a-way be-yond the blue

The joy had made her tongue feel thick and gave the preacher's wife a fuzzy face. But nothing tugged her back to stay among the grinning men and the smoke, nothing strong enough for that the more the women clapped to see the dress take shape. The more they laughed and sang and gave her presents when the dress was done.

"It's beautiful, Judy. Simply beautiful."

"That train shines like silver—look—see how it picks

up the light?"

"But isn't there a veil? Where's the veil?"

"Here—I fixed it yesterday. I wore it when I took my final vows."

And she had turned around and two or three times so they all could see, the preacher's wife a smiling face by then among the rest, all clear of joy-fuzz and the room so bright it made the air seem solid to the touch. The dress had rustled as she moved, the sound like paper crinkling in among the clapping hands and giggles there, her bulging front not near so fat-and-ugly, nothing near to what it was in waddle-walking or when she sat down to rest. The preacher's wife, Maybelle Manatee, had helped her down, with Big Nurse close beside, a crinkle and a squeak of silk and slowly to the middle of the room.

"This is Maybelle Manatee, Judy. Her husband will be tying the knot."

"That silk is just beautiful. And the lace—I haven't seen any lace like that for years."

"Did you notice how it shines—the train? See? The light looks like it's caught along the edges. Doesn't it look like it's caught there—like it's gotten down inside?"

"You're a beautiful bride, Judy. May God bless and—"

"Wait—the veil! Here—here—let me put it on—there—yes—now look—just look!"

"Beautiful! So very very beautiful."

The fiddle played alone, no singing with it now but loud enough and fast, a strong tune there to keep the dance alive. Maybelle shuffle-stepping with her cowboy boots a heel-and-toe gone quick down on the stage.

The Hoppers and the Big Boys were nearly with her beat for beat, all whoop and squeal and bellow rising through the air. Judy shifted in her chair and pushed the nearest plate away, still almost covered by a slice of turkey and a chunk of sugared ham, the special food that Emment somehow found, and two half-eaten rolls and stuffing filled with chestnuts sliced up fine and one short glass of joy near empty there beside the crystal butterfly that Big Nurse gave her when they got back to the Guest House for the night.

"This was my mother's—but I want you to have it. He loves you, Judy. He really does. I know that now. I've seen it grow—day by day. His love."

"I—I know. And I love him too."

"Yes. Yes, I think maybe you really do. I didn't at first. I thought a lot of things at first. But you're still here. You didn't run away. And he's a man that needs that more than most. People that'll stay with him."

And Big Nurse kissed her on the cheek, just like she did this afternoon, back when the preacher took his place across the room from where they put the table and the stage, the room all covered over nearly everywhere she looked with paper flowers and the popcorn ropes the Big Boys like to make. Big Nurse kissed her and the old man, Emment, walked beside her through the children on both sides behind the boy-girl Hopper, Gemma-Girl and Jesse-Lee, with paper flowers dropping down a crunch and scrape beneath her slippered feet. The fiddle there up high and higher than the rest, a scrape and twitch of music reaching toward the open beams of wood above their heads, a skipping march of sound from where the preacher's wife swayed in her little shuffle-dance raised up near the wall, her stage a stack of tumble-mats. Then Parker stepping out around the Torsos on their carts, the Fun-Heads in a close and sucking sound across the way, near to the preacher in his shiny suit and beaded string-tie held together by a turquoise dove. The fiddle stopped, its last note dropped away and lost and Gemma-Girl and Jesse-Lee pushed in to stand down at the Big Boys' knees while other Hoppers, Two-Hands and the One-Eyes too all hummed and chirped among the nuns and what they held up high to see, the bits-and-pieces in their arms, the almost-come-together babies there and clicking in a trill and rolling cluck-cluck-cluck like chickens come at last out to the rising of the sun. And every one was there it seemed, each one a different sound and come together many more than she had seen and listened to at FirstLight or at EveningSing.

The preacher's voice had come in like a shout:

"Brothers and sisters re-joice! Again I say it—re-joice! Re-joice—re-joice in the Lord always!"

And all the baby-noise, the children's voices great and small, in grunt and bird-shriek, dove-moan and in half-words hummed, a rise and fall of something like a song come in to join the preacher's own high voice and upraised arms that made the Bible that he held seem jumped to life, a flapping thing with thick black wings gone beating up and down and just about to fly away.

O nananana como ah ladanda
Landanda malanola danda lacola

The preacher's face had been a mass of wrinkles, dark skin glistened over from the sweat that curled and ran like creeks in springtime, like the mountain gullies deep within the greening-time and filled with water blinking in a sparkle-shine and glow. And she had tried to understand his words but nothing much came clear and Parker reached to take her hand, hard pressing on her wrist until their fingers met.

O Malanda ladanda comananana

The children all had seemed to join the preacher-song, the Bible-bird flapping harder and the fiddle back and squawking in a shrill and jump and somewhere deep inside it all she thought she heard the little voice rise up to buzz its bee-sing rich and full.

Mmmmmmmmmmmmmmmmm

Then gone away then come back stronger than before, then staying for awhile and mixed in with the preacher and the rest, a flicker there like candle-shadow out across each face, a dancing skitter on and on that made her touch the fat-and-ugly, hand a shake and fingers pressing gently just so see if it was there.

Mmmmmmmmmmmmmmmmm

The preacher stopped his song, had brought it down with 'amens' there, with 'praise the Lords' thrown in between each word he tried to speak, on down and down until the Bible-bird had roosted in his lowered hands, its wings bent back and belly white and shining in the light. And Parker, tall above her in a smile that twitched his crooked nose, his face as dark almost as what the preacher showed but more red in the cheeks and on the skin his collar touched, hand tight about her own and body pressed in close a comfort warm and safe. The preacher nearly shouted out the words.

"This is a ho-ly union—a ho-ly thing we see! No matter how it came to be—No matter what has come before! A ho-ly joining man to woman in the blessed sight a God!"

And readings from the Bird, of Cana and a wedding-feast and God's name there among it all and hers and Parker's too and words to say together and alone. And all the children chirped or sucked in air, full gurgled or squawked out loud, a dove-moan—cattle-bawl and one lone bellow from the biggest Big Boy there. And boy-girl Hopper, Gemma-Girl and Jesse-Lee a bounce and squeak just like a rubber toy. And Parker squeezing on her hand.

But somehow there inside each sound, for her alone it seemed grown sad among the rest, the deep and humming bee-sing all around and Medix strong and come down full upon it all, down like a mountain fog or what had spread itself in stench that one day out across the swamp. The last one clear each time she shut her eyes, the DOCTOR and the NURSE, there once again and words and words and words all given with a soothing smile and gentle pat upon her arm in walking to that room, the one all polished steel and sparkling tubes and table fitted to her back and hips, the smiles and gentle words and Daddy's laugh and Copper's too like dogs far off and barking at the night.

The DOCTOR first:

Are we ready, Ms. Taylor?

And then the NURSE:

Think about that new bikini, honey—Just keep your mind on that.

And then the thing itself, not ever clear and she had tried and tried to make it so, had tried but never even dreamed it back to life, just over in a hum and hum and hum and nothing else but that, a hum and hum and dreaming later of the voice, of voices way back to the mountain and the first one gone away but one voice left like all the rest had come inside it in a buzz that joined to bump and tumble, rise and fall and call out to her in the dark.

Mmmmmmmmmmmmmmmmmmmmm

A call cut through the NoFuss shots and packets full of condoms and the little pills and Mmmmmmm a stronger calling through it all she now could see, back through it all and lost until she felt the squeeze of Parker's hand and opened up her eyes to see a ring held up by Jesse-Lee.

#

Big Nurse and the nun were putting up their brooms, the rice all gone from where the Big Boys dropped the bags when everything was done. And Parker's lips had felt like fire upon her own and fat-and-ugly went away when he had held her tight. The fiddle had come in and strong, the preacher and the Big Boys dancing arm-in-arm, and food and words and singing too, the tables filled and clatter all around. And then the preacher's wife had played the children off to bed, with just the Hoppers with her on the stage and Big Boys down below, the oldest leaving last and now the fiddle slowing to a stop, a buzz behind it soft then stronger, something nearly clear to sight and Parker and the preacher coming in the door.

CHAPTER TWELVE

Doc had smelled of tar right at the first, the first-pain now a blessed thing beside what came—again—again—again—then rest and try to breathe—try and try and then again and push-again and something on her forehead wet and cooling like the spring rain on the mountain, and again—again—again—her back so tired and achy—tired and paining her like when she—again—again—like when she danced that dog-bump, pony-trotting thing, that hard bump roll and slow bump two and three and two and three and bump it baby bump it slow and easy baby bump it hard and God O God—again—again—again—and quicker now and hot knife hot—knife blade in deep deep deep and twist it baby oh my—like that bumping thing the ac/dcs loved to see—and words come calling out across the speckled light—again—red in it deep and streaky, streaky streak and black—again

Judy—Judy—almost done

Doc smelled of tar at first and then like vodka in her glass—again—again—oh God—again—like vodka—push-down push-down push and push—breathe a wet a—sweet God just a taste of something—now and now—and push and push—again—again—sweet Jesus just a drop down on her tongue—her tongue—the streaky and the red and black the strongest now—the black across it all across the push and deep—again and taking off the rest, across her eyes so hard she seemed to fall down in it as it passed, down sucked inside and nothing there but falling-time and deep and back and back and full away—back from the push-again and what the first-pain set to burning—back to the fat-and-ugly rising up like morning back and back and through it all—again—the words turned tiny and then gone away.

Judy—Judy—don't—Judy

A black a blackness there but not so deep and her outside herself somehow, and inside too, a dream but not like all the rest: a moving backwards through it all and streaky red in speckled light around the inside-outside shes, the moving shes that felt each bump and little rock there on the road.

The fat-and-ugly first of all, like Doc's first smell and more, of tar and stale and everything, each smell and twitch of pain a living thing, the outside watching what the inside had to do, the tired-out waddle and the belly-hurt, the belly tender like a bruise too deep to paint away. The fat-and-ugly month on month to never end it seemed, back back and just a half-step close enough to hear the words beyond.

Judy—push now—push—again—now

But fat-and-ugly and gone back again, down in the dark and streaky red, back through the tired and achy, sick like nothing else could do, the morning sick and afternoon and night sometimes all ready set to die right into sleep, she tumbled now back through it all—again.

Judy—Judy—push—push—now

And then the fat-and-ugly gone away, dropped off like clothes at night, and dancing now a rolling flashing Beaver-time and raised up slow and full on through the streaky, through the red and outside with the inside now a dance a bump and—push—push—bump and roll and grinding with the music there, the music Copper liked the best and voices there in speckled light not Doc or

Big Nurse or the worried one that Parker sometimes was—push—and push—again—again—not any one of those—not one—but Copper-sounding when she knew for sure, not fat-and-ugly like she got, not yet like that at all and Copper-sounding spit and hiss come out his mouth come out and mixed in with the words he yelled come out come out come out to play again—again—come out to rip and tear again—come out come out again.

"Bitch! Go'damned bitch—bitch!"

And more and more and fat-and-ugly hiding inside ready to come out and out but not like later not like when she'd run away for good.

"Bitch—you—damn you—I can't re-place you now—an' you know it too—not now—you will go back go'damn you—you will go back!"

But Copper floating to the side and round and round and Medix up and quick-flashed deep inside a water black and streaky red and Copper floating in it bob and dunk and then the NURSE popped out not with a smile or eyes that even move, the NURSE a piece of paper in her hand and humming back behind her desk and humming back down past the swinging doors and hum and buzz there too a little bit a buzz and everything a whirl and whirl around around a whirl like water in a tub, a water-whirl all draining down and gone.

Judy—Judy can you hear me? Can you hear?

Then deeper in and floating now the inside-outside bobbing down the drain a humming down inside a sparkle-drain and pipe and out the other side and out popped out the other side and fat-and-ugly solid gone—push—push she still can hear them but from far away a nearer push and push down in her now and out upon a blanket on the sand, out from the sparkle-drain and pipe and ocean-sound so close it's like a shell held to her ear, so close and in and out and inandout and push push wait and weight upon her one by one they drop down on her down on where the fat-and-ugly waits to show and squish and squish and just a little push-apart of streaky red and moonlight moon and silver and a grinning face there up above a grin and gone a grinning face and faces there man-in-the-moon and in and out and inandout inandout inandout her hips a bang and bump and scrape across the blanket on the sand.

"Just—a—lit-tle—lon-ger—oh—"

"I'm next—me—me—not you—not—"

"You take too damned long!"

"What's she sayin'? Can you hear it?"

"Nothin'—I don't hear nothin'."

"There—ain't she tryin' t'say somethin'?"

"It's my turn—dammit it's my turn!"

"Somebody hold her head—hold it—"

"She is talkin'—and—and biting again!"

"Sit on her head—there—mind them teeth—hold her now—hold her—"

"Give her 'nother drink—here—give her this—"

And hot and hotter in her throat and sweet but dry and hot and cool and wet again all on her forehead and her face her eyes and heavy on her head and push and push and Parker's voice too far away too far away and tiny now and GodohGodohGod and push push push again—again—again—and inside-outside under deep and under deep deep deep and heavy hard down on the in and out and inandout and near to ripping more and more and deep-filled and then gone to less and little tiny inandout a tickle in between her legs a moan of achy and man-in-the-moon and moon and ocean come together in a roar gone close and cold gone roaring ocean-sound and moon shell-caught a bee-sing in the sea-oats on a wind from far away—again—again—again

Just one more time—Judy? Judy can you hear me? Push now push—push—more and more--push

Alone then all alone and speckled light from where the moon and ocean roared so close and cold together and the bee-sing seaoat-caught and wind a ripple on her legs so achy and a buzzing louder coming louder like the hiss and pop of fire the other way in Parker's room the others coming all in close and mixed into a single buzz again, a bee-sing with a face that she could almost see.

It—it's coming, Judy—the head—push—a pretty head—push—push again

The bee-sing standing in the air—push—ohGodohGodohGod—push—a shape a flicker like the shadows of a fire come up from deep inside a burning place and DOCTOR-DOCTORNURSE and DOCTORDOCTORNURSE and NURSE and hum and crackle of the fire behind but not there hot enough to stop its bee-sing buzz the mmmm-ing of a face and arms and legs and torso come to float upon the moon-and-ocean roaring roar and roaring on and on around and through it words now clear and tearing at her deep and lonely in the place she thought was lost and gone.

We sing

Then sounds the mmmm gone from them and a feel

of wet and cool and just a touch upon her lips a wipe and gone and ohGod push and push again—again the bee-sing never coming back a sweep up from the sand and through it all again again again the face for just a second there walking on the air the wind blew in all cool and then turned warm and gone and gone away the face and little body on the empty air a smile that seemed to touch and fill her with its joy—

And back to Parker then—and back and back to where it all began—to Parker's face above and Doc a pine-tar smell down where she couldn't see—

There! Would you look at that? My God look at it—it's—it's a girl, Judy—a girl!

CHAPTER THIRTEEN—FRAGMENTS

-1-

Buster Welborne smiled and raised his hands to grip the padded steering-wheel. The truck was new. A DIAL-A-BORT Deluxe with storage tank the biggest in the fleet. And freshly washed and waxed that afternoon. The cab was wide and deep with four seats and a sleeper back behind. His own chair swiveled and it felt like silk, deep plush and fitted to the way he liked to sit. The dash glowed green and the radio sent out a soothing hum and sometimes murmur when a call came in. He flexed his fingers slow and let them come down one by one upon the wheel again and tapping with the beat the in-cab stereo put out. It had been a busy night. Four calls along the Rainbow Strip, the Silver Beaver twice and one quick 'public service' at the County Jail. The Triple-X was taking longer than he thought it would, the three attendants gone an hour now, leaving him with nothing much to do but play his music and watch the limos come and go. The big cars with the girls in fur and men sometimes so fat he wondered how they got inside.

He cracked the window and then brushed a few times at the silver braid along his sleeves. The jumpsuit was new, the latest style and smelled like leather. A good smell, rich and full and nothing like the Medix-stench or old man Cutter's pickles as he bent to come down close. A good rich smell instead and soft, no special gear to hurt his chest or oven heat to blister up his skin or ringing telephones to make him want to scream. He liked the way the fabric felt and how the silver sometimes sparkled in the light. His girlfriend made him wear it when he took her out. He smiled again and settled deeper in the chair. The Triple-X was sure to finish out his shift.

Someone shouted something, a scream-like echo just behind it toward the Funhouse ramp, the sound enough to cut clean through his latest DeadWitch song. He buzzed the window open, full open now and cold air like a slap across his face. A red-headed woman was out there running up the ramp, her scream the echo to the men not far behind, the Strip Police in full-dress uniform and shiny boots and catching-nets swung high and wide to bring her down. Buster yawned and buzzed the window shut. The second-shift was mostly fun, the early night not messy like it got past one o'clock. Not like his first week on the job when all he did was drive the Welfare Crew. Back roads and shacks. The scrawny women in those chutes the county used, lined up and packed all tight inside the Freedom Tents and each one with an R&I, a free ride on the green-paged Rape and Incest forms the county boys gave out to everyone who asked. Green paper there in every scrawny hand and waiting in the chutes for hours at a time. The attendants always came back smelling like they'd rolled in something dead. And no one laughed or joked or shared a pint, the drive out to Disposal nothing like it was on first or second shift. No fun at all. But even third-shift driving beat the PhoneBank booths. And Welfare stink had never even made it close to what he'd dug through in that Medix shovel job. That smell that nothing ever washed away. The Strip Police had slung the red-headed woman on a Party-Pole, net bucking as she kicked and rolled from side to side, her screams just barely getting through the DeadWitch 'lullaby.' He liked that song the best. He wondered what the girl had failed to do.

Inna inna down—oh yeah—bay-bee
inna inna down-you—inna inna you
inna you
inna you
down down inna-you inna bay-bee you

The attendants were taking longer than he thought they would. The call had been for four quick-sux and thirteen cheeses (rind-cores with the latest rotors) and a sux-bath for a politician's wife. Nothing special there at all. And the Triple-X was built to make it quick, smooth and quick in special rooms down hallways back behind the walls. But the attendants were still trainees, first time on their own and not yet sure enough for speed. The shift was almost over and Buster thought about his girl, long legs and tits that made him squirm just thinking about how they looked. The kind that pushed up and the nipples nearly always tight and stiff. She worked at Condom City on the three-to-midnight run, Complaints Department secretary with a raise and two-weeks paid vacation every year. He had met her at the Silver Beaver on the singles-only night. Six months before his driving job came through. Before his cousin got the dispatch job and signed him on. And she had moved in with him just last week (after months of back-and-forth between his place and hers), into his cottage near the Mall that had a swimming pool out back and double laundry room. A two-car garage and a sundeck too and furnished like the places in the magazines. He liked it very much.

Inna inna—you my bay-bee bay-bee
Inna-you inna inna-you
you---you---you

Deadwitch was his favorite band and 'lullaby' the best song they ever did. She liked it too. Corinne Massey. She said she came from Mississippi. Somewhere like that. And that her name was Corinne Massey. And the Condom City job was the best one she had ever had. Like his driving for DIAL-A-BORT. The best job there was. Free from trough-stink and the stuff that never would wash out. Free from old man Cutter and the phones that never quit. The best job ever.

Inna inna inna you
bay-bee bay-bee you you you
inna inna in you you
bay-bee bay-bee inna-you

And she was clean too oh God yes clean as anything. NoFuss safe and her health card punched right on the money, right on the due date every month, all checked out class-A clean. She tasted like a salty drink. But something in it sweet and smelling nice the times she let him use his tongue. Clean like nothing else he'd ever tasted. And smart too. Long black curly hair and tits that made him squirm to see her let them out. Short-breathed then and aching low and hard. She was smart too. Read books sometimes. Whole books the kind with covers on them. Hard covers. And legs so long they made him nearly lose it watching when she put on hose. The kind he liked the most. Black silk and fancy garters like the B-Girls wore. She made him help her snap them on sometimes. Just for fun. And sometimes got dressed up in his uniform and played around, like she was driving out to give a quick-sux or a cheese. They laughed a lot together when they stayed at home.

in in
in in
in in
Y-O-U

The last tune was mostly shrieks and screams and something like a hammer beating on a steak. The Witch was really good and Corinne sometimes made him turn it up loud when they fucked. She liked that word a lot but never used it in a crowd. She said she liked the way it felt to say it just to him alone. She liked to sing and cook and crawl up in the sleeper of the truck when he could keep it overnight. They fucked a lot out there until it got too cold. He tapped the wheel and tried to keep up with the hammer blows. The boom-a-splat boom-splat—sh-sh-sh gone faster toward the end and buzzing there like rattlesnakes down in a pit. He said the word himself and closed his eyes and let the tits come free and bounce down on his chest.

"Osborne—hey!"

Buster jumped and buzzed open the window. The attendant was upset, the fat one. Buster couldn't see the other two, most likely already squeezed into the follow-up van. The fat attendant sounded out of breath, his face all wet and shiny in the neon light. His white gloves were stained, every finger splotched and dark. A hundred dollar fine if he got caught.

"What?"

"Start it up, Osborne—we're done."

"About time—what took so long?"

"Just start it!"

"And them stains. That'll cost you if the—"

"Just start it up! Ok? God what a night—start it Osborne start it!"

"Sure sure—"

And Buster flipped the suction switch and settled back to let the motor start its climb—pressure gauge gone brighter green and numbers flashing by—10—20—30—up to 50 quick and on to 60—70—80 and the bright red 100 beeping as he pulled the intake lever down. He stuck his head outside and stretched to see the rolling tanks, tops gleaming, locked-in flush and set to go, the hoses down below and slowly coming up to even pressure with the truck. The fat attendant wiped his face with a red handkerchief and rubbed the back of his neck. He looked like he was sick.

"You Ok?"

"Yeah."

"You want sit in here with me an' wait?"

"I said I'm Ok."

Buster shrugged and settled back behind the wheel. The Witch was slowing down. The last tune ending with a clack and rattle like a bag of bones. A long black limo pulled up to the entrance of the Triple-X. The driver got out quick and ran around to open up the right-hand door. His uniform was full of sparkles in the light, like gold there glinting as he moved. Buster hummed the Witch away and watched the long-legged woman stepping out.

-2-

The Bowman's arm was getting tired. The wind had strengthened with a sting of ice in every gust and night was nearly come. He had tried the shot from every blind, palmetto-thicket to the pines and back across the marsh, mud everywhere they stepped and grass all slick and wet, the old man with the shotgun firing wide one time but two more there so close they chopped the clay beside the Bowman's feet. He crouched behind a cedar bush and pinged the flamer on its way, a tumbled loop that hit the wind all wrong.

"Lost it again, Pa. Way wide."

"Yeah."

The boy had kept up pretty good so far, his first trip out for pay and two shots yesterday the boss-man saw and liked. But nothing much had worked today, no contact anywhere and flamer after flamer knocked off by the wind. The boy had seemed to sink down in himself all afternoon, not saying much and eyes gone sometimes wide and staring at the misses and the mess. It made the Bowman think how he himself had likely looked and done back when his Daddy took him out to work. The Bowman slid another flamer in the Agincourt, his Daddy's favorite bow and notched along the stock for every barn and silo he had burned.

"What is that thing anyways, Pa? Some kind of g'rage?"

"Chicken house."

"Chicken house?"

"Yeah."

"It don't look like no chicken house."

"Well it is. Or was. That there's a old-timey one. Used t'all be three stories high down in the country. Long time ago."

The boy knelt down to wrap some arrows, his fingers quick and sure and kerosene smell strong until he capped his flask. They'd have enough to last until the sun was gone and maybe just a few left over for a closer run. The boss-man wanted that chicken house today, an extra hundred dollars' worth and whiskey too, a jug of Georgia corn.

"Wind's too high t'hit it, Pa. We too far away."

"I can get it, boy. Need to put me one in that hole up yonder by that feed-tank on th'roof. That there's th'place a'right. It'll go then. I know it."

The Bowman pinged another flamer high this time and pointed at the left, a sweep that caught the wind and rode it tumbling at the last and down too fast and gone. His arms were tired and his fingers were cut across the tips, his gloves not helping anything and the chicken house still there and shotgun blast a rip and crashing through some nearby pines.

"He's 'bout got us pegged in again, Pa."

"I know it."

"We goin' over to th'oaks this time?"

"Just hush now, boy. Just be still."

It had gone much better yesterday, the wind too weak and fog rolled in by noon. The boy had helped him with the barn, his two rounds close behind the flamer that had hit, dead center of the roof with two caps set to blow as soon as they bumped down. The flame had shot up like a rocket's tail, deep red and blue and orange on the edges and the roof had tumbled in so quick it seemed an eye-blink would have missed it clean. The near woods fanned up in a roar of black smoke then and whip and curl of red-licks rising on the wind, a rise and fall and rise and fall just like the old days when his

Daddy rode the circuit and the black smoke curled and boiled behind him and the flames cut through the night, a burning-time come close and hot and bright as day. And shouting too, the part the Bowman liked the best, to hide and hear the screams and shrieks, the whoops and yells and all the rest, the shadows flickered on the air and everywhere the jump-and-run, the running all around a dancing there close by the fire and feeling deep inside his belly all warm and like a woman soft and welcome to him in the deep of night. The boy had done it good and he had seen it on his face, the grin and eyes like tears about to come and shifting foot to foot upon the clay. The boss-man had been there to see the shots, the fat boss in the fancy suit that paid the money right up front and promised more when everything got done.

"Getting' late, Pa. Sun's most gone."

"I know that, boy. I can see it plain."

The boy was started straight as he could go, already far past where the Bowman was when he had been thirteen.

The Bowman slipped the arrow into place, the Agincourt all smooth and steady on the pull-back and the safety clicking right. He pushed the shaft in close against the wood and flared the cloth to help the fire take hold. The lighter hissed and popped along the side and dropped down dangling on its chain. He liked the whoosh and flap-flap-flap the flamer made, the arrow's tip a stab of blue-and-yellow raised up in a single sweep and gone.

"Got it, Pa! Look! Whew—gone!"

And whoosh-pop whoosh and roar across the roof

just like a blanket there unrolling middle to the sides, the feed-tank one thick bar of flame and smoke begun to boil and whip down to the ground. The Bowman smiled and licked his lips, salty tasting in the warmer wind, the shotgun blasting twice to trouble nothing but some marsh grass further in. The sun was almost down.

"What's that, Pa? Is it birds? Are they chickens out there in that—"

"Just hush, boy. Be still an' lissen. Shut your eyes and lissen."

The Bowman knelt down slow and careful on the clay, his eyes closed tight and face turned toward the fire. The shrieks and screams and yells were louder now, come on the wind a cry like babies frightened and alone. He'd buy the boy a dinner when they got back into town. And save the jug of whiskey for the long drive home.

-3-

Mr. Cibber had barely touched his food, the Combination Plate still full of baby shrimp and something like a crab down in the French-fries near the slaw. The 'Neptune Room' was filled with booths and fish net dangled from the ceiling beams; aquariums were set in every wall and up behind the bar and someone kept on shouting, high and sing-song in among a clank and crash of dishes every time a waiter shuffled-stepped back through the swinging kitchen doors. A candle flickered down inside a shell-encrusted globe, off-center on the table and pushed hard between a mound of empty oyster shells and little bowls of dark and gummy rice. Mr. Shadwell sucked down another oyster and sighed. He had swallowed twenty by the time their dinner order came and Mr. Cibber quit counting.

It was crowded when they first came in but now the sailors at the bar had left and almost every Shriner too, the Lions Club had filed out from a curtained corner near the door and right behind them fourteen dwarfs in baseball caps and wearing tasseled vests and buckskin pants had piggy-backed it from the far wall booths and sang a song in German while they paid their bill. Mr. Shadwell had clapped and sucked in another oyster when the dwarfs had galloped out the door.

“Excellent, Cibber—they must be salesmen, don’t you think?”

But Mr. Cibber had said nothing in reply, pushing shrimp and other fried things round and round on his plate instead, the crab gone hiding and come back with little eyes, three of them or maybe four like polished beads, and bits of slaw and French-fries clinging to its claws. CAP’N CRAWDAD’S CABIN was Mr. Shadwell’s favorite place to eat. All local seafood and the drinks were strong.

“I’ve never tasted better, Cibber. Never. I know I know—atrocious ambiance—I know. Franchise—uh—what did you call it?”

“Decadent.”

“Yes! Franchise-Decadent—yes—and it is. Yes yes. But not the food. Nothing disappointing there at all, eh?”

“Careful of your sleeve, Thomas.”

“Eh? What?”

“Your sleeve—the ‘Bayou Baste’ there—the bowl?”

“What? Oh—oh yes. Thank you. Did you try any of this?”

“No.”

"What?"

"I didn't try any."

"Oh. Too bad. But, Calvin—you've not eaten all your shrimp. And the 'Crab Maman'—there's raisin stuffing in that thing, you know. And heart of palm—diced with 'Peppers Lafitte'—an Anglo-Cajun specialty. Capn's own recipe."

"I'm—I'm not very hungry."

"Well you can at least eat the shrimp—try the 'Bayou Baste' with them—here let me spoon you a—"

"No! No—no really—I'm full."

"Ah—well—I feel good, Calvin. Yes indeed. It's nearly over. At last, eh?"

"Yes."

The sing-song shouting turned up louder, Shadwell sucking yet another oyster, purple with a stripe of red down through it like the others waiting in their half-shells on his plate. The mound of empty shells was taller than the candle-globe. Mr. Cibber wanted to go home, back to the penthouse at the Triple-X and back clean back to Charleston and an evening at the Club. A quiet evening in among the books and etchings there, the marble sculpture and the rubbings and the fine old wine they served him by the fire. The project here had gone on longer than he thought it would. But maybe it was finally ending after all.

"Over and done with. Ah me." Shadwell forked a bit of darkish rice into his mouth to chase another oyster down. "Ummm. Yes. I personally think Sledge will run. And soon."

"Run?"

"Yes. And leave the whole thing behind him. Whatever's left of it."

"The fires?"

"Yes yes. Unfortunate run of bad luck, eh? A terrible thing. Terrible. I hear there're just the central buildings left intact."

"The brick ones?"

"Don't look so worried, Calvin. Your brick is safe."

"That brick is valuable, Thomas—it's—it's—"

"Yes yes I know. And safe. But I hear it's gotten pretty bad out there. The fires are only a part of the bad luck. No more airlifts. No more food allotment. They're most likely reduced to eating roots by now. Most unfortunate. Yes. And so it goes, eh? I mean—we have tried to be reasonable. And generous. Every possible consideration was taken before—before the—uh—specialists were called in. And who knows—he might very well be selling diseased organs, Calvin. I only suggested that he could be—and it was only a passing thought. Social brainstorming with my government friends, you might say. A stray thought. But—well it might just be true. As true as all the rest."

"The rumors?"

"Some might call them that—yes. But they might just be true as well. There's the possibility of truth in every one. And that's a kind of truth, isn't it? Possible truth? Yes? Yes—and it worked. Much better than the earlier methods. The Homma Brothers. The Prospectus. The melodrama. All effective, of course, but only to a point. My own ideas were sounder in the home-stretch, I think. Established traditions. The older methods. Regional talent."

"I see."

"Yes—and Division East is quite pleased."

"And you think Sledge himself will run?"

"Oh yes—and soon."

"Alone then?"

"Oh—well—perhaps he'll take the girl. You know," he winked and raised an oyster shell carefully to his lips and sucked loudly. The pile of empty half-shells kept growing. He dabbed at his lips with a well-used napkin. "Ah—yes—the girl. An early disappointment. Friend Copper thought that we could use her—as a spy or something like that. Pretty silly stuff to look back on. She was pregnant, you know."

"No—but—"

"Silly all silly as can be. The Coppers are all alike. I'm sorry I even listened. All that wasted time. And effort. Health Department favors gone forever now. IOU's called in. Sledge knows the law. There was nothing there for us at all. Too messy and too loud to go the distance now. Too late to make it work. That second judge went soft and nobody local wants to touch it any more. The Sheriff least of all. He'd rather look the other way. But in spite of them every one," he winked again and squeezed the napkin, "the time has come round at last. A fearful thing, fire. Fearful. But so is sickness—pestilence, eh? Fearful. And there's nothing better than a fire for that—to stop it—if it's really there. Nothing better, eh?"

"They think Sledge is burning his own—"

"Rumors, Cibber, rumors. But it is still the best way to go—to stop a plague. And the place *is* burning down. Bit by bit. And there *are* Public Disposal Fugitives out there, yes? You saw them yourself, Cibber. Remember?"

"Yes."

"And who knows what they are capable of? Right? So it's best to keep it all there. Contained. Until the fire can do its job. That's why our friends are camped out in the woods. The Social Health and Welfare Volunteers. To watch the fires and not let anything crawl out. They've only just begun to help, you know. And all for free. And minimal outlay for the rest. For consultations. The specialists. A minimal expense. But then—you can't really put a price-tag on regional traditions, can you? Do try the 'Bayou Baste', Calvin. It's especially delicious with shrimp."

"No. I've had enough."

"Well. And your Aztec?"

"Pardon?"

"Your Aztec? Totally approved, I presume. Your final plans?"

"Oh. Yes. Yesterday."

"Excellent news. You see, I told you everything would come in right on time. Remember?"

"Yes. And Sledge will run?"

"Like a rabbit if he has any sense at all. And the girl with him, I suppose. And then the rest. The other men and women there. When they discover that he's gone. The PDFs will be the easy part. They can't go with him anyway. They'll only slow him down and make it easy for the Volunteers. He knows all that. I'm sure he does. And so he'll run. Like you. Like me. Like anyone would do. He knows alone he's got a chance to get away. And then the local law can act. Without that second judge. For special-handling. Forfeiture of land and property.

Human disposal and public auction. And everything as legal as can be."

"But—but what if he doesn't run?"

Mr. Shadwell tapped his fork tines on the mound of oyster shells, a few quick clicks that tumbled down the top ones in a slide that rocked the bowls of rice. His eyes were sparkling in the candlelight. "Ah yes. The foolish possibility. The sad alternative." He shook his head and dropped the fork beside his plate. "If he stays—we'll simply save what brick we can, eh?"

The sing-song shouting lost itself down in crash of pots and clanking like a chain pulled hard across a wooden floor. Mr. Shadwell sighed and pushed back in his chair. The crab on Mr. Cibber's plate was halfway up a tangled stack of fries, its claws deep in the slaw and its tiny eyes fixed steady on the fishnets overhead.

-4-

The coals were shimmer-hot and sizzling with spots of fat down on them that sent smoke-wisps up to curl about the roasting meat. The men were huddled close, a lightly misting rain come in and ground-fog in behind that boiled and drifted through the pines and grass and made the tents look slick as seal-skin, several of them glowing from the lantern light inside, a jagged line that stretched back out of sight. From time to time, the men would hold out slabs of thick bread underneath the meat to catch a bit of dripping fat. A stack of crudely lettered signs lay on a folded tarp and somewhere in the distance toward he east, out where the sky was always brushed with red, a siren sounded and a horn, long blasts that echoed faintly in a wobbling cry like dogs in sudden pain.

"What is that thing anyways?"

"Burky caught it s'afternoon—ain't that right, Burky?"

"Yeah."

"He says it's some kind a fish. Hey—where's th'Barrow boys an' Bug? You seen 'em, Burky?"

"Yeah. They ain't hungry. Say they ain't anyways. Gone on to the tents, I reckon."

"This here don't taste like no fish."

"Well Burky says it sure come up like one."

"Don't look like no fish neither."

"What was that y'call it, Burky? Y'know—when y'brung it in—that name y'called?"

"Mudfish."

"Yeah. Mudfish. He says it's a mud-fish."

"Well it don't look like no kind a fish I ever seen. An' it sure's hell don't taste like no fish."

"Don't eat none then."

"There somethin' else here t'eat is they?"

"No they ain't. Groc'ry run ain't till tomorra. Bug's ol' woman's drivin' in."

"Then I'll eat it. But it still look funny. Tastes like pig fat t'me."

"It's a mudfish. Ain't no pig can swim under the damned water. I caught mudfish lots a times down home."

"Burky's a swamp man, y'see—an' he knows his fish—right, Burky?"

"Then what's that thing on th'side there? Looks like a lil' ol' foot there—see it? Ain't that a foot? Toes? What y'suppose it do wif feet?"

"Hey—ya'll did gut this thing, didn't ya?"

"Hell yes I gutted it! Burky catched it an' I gutted it. An' done right too. Y'ain't gotta eat none if it bother you so damn much!"

"Ain't said I won't eat it. Just look funny. An'—an' it ain't got no fish smell to it at all."

"How long 'fore she's done, Burky?"

"'Bout there now."

"See—that's how she smells when she's done."

"Where y'say y'got it anyway?"

"Back yonder."

"Down in that swamp? Down there?"

"Yeah."

"Shit—that place smell like a toilet. Hey—you see any a them monsters out there? We was workin' th'fence most of th'day—they ain't tried nothin' is they? Since them fires burn out? Y'see any a 'em back there in that swamp?"

"Too foggy t'see much a nothin'."

"Yeah. Like th'fence—nothin' movin' no more. Think they all dead in there?"

"Maybe. Maybe not. There'll come a clearin' in a day or two. Then we can see."

"Hope t'hell that shotgun's dead."

"What 'zactly they got in there anyways?"

"I heard it's like that shit th'faggots usta get—ya'll hear that?"

"Yeah."

"Only worse'n that. Puts blisters on ya. Burns ya skin. An' hits th'lil' chil'ren worse'n anybody. Poor lil' chil'ren—an' kills 'em quick too I hear."

"I heard they can breath it on ya. Do it like that. Suppose that's so?"

"Well I ain't gettin' closte enough t'find out."

"How it get started anyways?"

"I heard that man done it—pullin' in sick babies—y'know—pullin' in them kind."

"Shit—ain't that 'gainst th'law? Ain't they suppose be let alone?"

"I ain't sure no more. But they all sick in there. I'm damn sure a that."

"Yeah. Everbody knows that."

"Yeah."

"Y'know—this here ain't bad tastin' on th'bread."

"If y'like pig fat it ain't."

"Hey Burky—ya really didn't see nothin' out there? In that swamp?"

"Nothin'. Just th'mudfish when I set th'hook. He come up quick."

The siren and the horn had stopped, a murmur now come softly from the darkened tents, behind the men a murmur and a stronger glowing in the sky above, a smear of throbbing red there in a rise and fall to match the glowing coals and spit and hiss of roasting meat.

-5-

Congee saw a face. The trough-lights bright and his shift about to end. The last quick sweep to feed the ovens one more time and done. But there it was, popped up like some potato in a stew, a bob and dunk and laying easy then a floater gentle as can be. It nearly made him drop his shovel.

"Johnny! Hey—hey Johnny!"

The face had seemed to smile, a curl about the lips and edges turning up to where some strings of hair had stuck. The cheeks were caught in hair, and ears peeped out like little wings to ride the waves his shovel made.

"Yo Johnny—dammit—Johnny!"

The face had eyes there too, wide open in a stare that seemed to take in everything above. Each time it stopped its bob and dunk. Each time it floated nearly still. Open eyes and smile and pointed at the trough-lights and at Congee too. It seemed like it was watching, waiting there awhile to see what he might do.

"Yo Johnny—"

"Hey man—easy—easy now. You want Boss Fuller hear all this here yellin'? He dock us if he do—"

"But look at that—that down there—it's—"

"Where?"

"Right there—there—see it?"

"Shit, man—I sees a sticker—chop it. Shift's most done."

"But—it—it's smilin', Johnny—that thing's smilin' at me!"

"Shit smilin', man. That's a sticker is all. Jus' a lil' ol' sticker. You seen 'em afore. You seen stickers ever night."

"Not—not like that I ain't. It—it's got eyes—"

"They all got 'em, man—what look like eyes anyways. But they jus' look like it—ain't real. Nothin' real 'bout it, man—you knows that. That there is a Noo Yawk sticker is all—whole damn shipment t'night's from up yonder. Noo Yawk. I seen th'trucks. Jus' chop it afore Boss Fuller look an' see us standin' 'round like this—jus' chop—"

"It—it's got hair, Johnny—it looks like it—it's alive down there—it—"

"Shit, man—lissen—you want me chop it f'ya? You

need he'p, boy? Want me t'do it? 'Cause y'gonna get us fired sure's hell standin' 'round like this here. Let ol' Johnny he'p ya now. Y'don't look so good—"

"No—look—look at that—ain't that a hand there—see it? It's got a neck too—chest—it's smilin' at me, Johnny—it's—"

"Go'dammit, boy—go'dammit it all—"

A chop-chop in the rolling soup and splash of sweet-smell up to cover Congee's arms, Black Johnny pushing short and quick, his shovel blade dropped down and one two three and hard. And soup gone all the same again. And oven doors clanked open for the roll and buck and slide. And Congee with his shovel all alone.

PART THREE

"One Welcome Child"

CHAPTER FOURTEEN

The man was slender and his trench-coat almost new. A khaki-colored coat and on his head a Stetson hat. And bearded face that glistened wet beneath the porch light at the door. He had carried the child for hours through the rain and mud. He said he'd left his car back near the highway, at the first bend in the road, a creek now crashing through and winding back and forth to chop away the gravel and the clay. A mile or more of sliding mud and churning water red and filled with brush. And snakes, he said, a few times clumps of them that tumbled bumped and twisted up to try and catch at something firm, to hold to something long enough to stop. He had the child beneath his coat, a head that poked up near the collar, one eye wide and staring from the middle of a greenish face.

The man had stumbled as he stepped into the room, the child a squeak and cluck-cluck digging tighter on his chest. The man had tried to smile as Parker led him over near what remained of the fire. Judy and the baby were in bed, both she and Crystal Bea asleep and breathing softly down among the blankets there. The man had taken off his hat and water-spray had hissed into the glowing coals.

"I've never seen anything like this before."

His voice was calm and low, a husky sound about the words like something was caught down in his throat. The child had clung hard to his chest the whole way in, he said, with fingers dug into his shirt and legs wrapped tight about his waist, not letting go no matter what had happened on the road and in the woods. Parker shook his head and dropped a slender log down on the coals.

"You see—I thought I'd hit it. Just popped up in my headlights. About ten miles out. I—I still don't see how I missed."

He'd passed a Kiddie Kuntry sign, an old one somehow left alone, and tried to get there in his car. Parker helped him with his coat and took his hat and patted at the child, a brush-away of water from its head and just a tiny squeeze upon its arm.

"I—I've been here before—years ago. When I worked for the old Slackbridge Reporter. It's gone now. The Reporter. But I did a story on this place. The wire services picked it up. It went all over. Do you remember me?"

"No—I don't think I do."

"Poretta? Rick Poretta? I sent you a copy of the feature. It's been—oh—ten years ago at least."

"Wait—yes. I do remember—but—you don't look—"

"The beard? It's still fairly new. I'm not used to it myself."

"I remember you. And the article. A good one."

The child had squeaked again and tried to climb higher on his chest. The man seemed about to fall.

"Let me help you—here—let me take the child."

"It's gotten heavier—it was no trouble at all at first—never made a sound in the car. All rolled up like a ball down on the floorboard. And it was very light to carry. At first it was very light—when I started in on foot. But now—"

And Parker pried it loose, its hands reached fast to take his shirt and hold on tighter than before, little legs and knees pressed hard about his waist. The man stepped to a nearby chair and sat down slowly. The child squeaked loud and tried to hide its face in Parker's shirt.

"This place has changed."

"Yes."

"I think I read something about it. Awhile back. Wire-service copy or something. But I didn't pay it much mind at the time. I was working on a story then. I'm still a reporter. In Atlanta now."

"I see. There-there. There-there."

The child was rocking slow in Parker's arms, the log flared brighter with a spray of sparkles toward the coal-bed glowing nearly red. And Crystal Bea began a cooing grunt, mixed in with Judy's snores and sudden tap-tap-tap of rain down on the tin roof overhead.

"Getting worse out there."

"Yes. There-there. He's steadying down now. He'll need to sleep."

"I—I almost hit it—almost killed it. Things happened so fast—one inch more and—"

"Were you going to Atlanta? Were you driving there?"

"What?"

"When you found him—this baby. Were you going home?"

"Oh—no. No I'm on assignment. Two weeks. I was on my way to Florida. A press convention in Jacksonville. It's really a kind of vacation though. I used to live there."

"I see."

"What happened here?"

"Pardon?"

The man had wiped at his beard with a shaking hand and turned sideways in the chair, facing toward the fire and glancing up at Parker and the child. The child seemed to copy Crystal Bea, a clucking-coo that rose and fell with Parker's breathing and the rain-tap on the roof.

"What happened?"

"We're leaving here. Tomorrow night."

"But why? Look—I saw it—all of it. The burned-out buildings. The men in the woods. They were armed. One of them even shot at me coming in. Why?"

The child cluck-cooed and Crystal Bea had answered, little grunts but quickly lost down in the snores from Judy, the hiss and crackle of the fire there too and tap-tap drill of rain and wind that banged a shutter somewhere like a gunshot or a crack of thunder near at hand. The child was sleeping now and Parker took it to the pallet, kneeling down to fix the blankets there all soft and let the green head bob a bit as it came in and slow and easy down to rest. The man stretched out his legs, ankles crossed and hands behind his head.

"What is it? That child—I've never seen one like it. Nothing like it—like him. You called it, him—green—his skin is—"

"He's a run-away. They do that sometimes."

"Then he's one of yours? The deformed—the mentally challenged—those children you keep here—the dumpster-babies—the ones I wrote about?"

"No. He's never been here. They sometimes lose them on the road."

"Who? Who loses them?"

"Transports. Disposal Units—Public Disposal—"

"The Landfill Law—the newest law? Is that it?"

"Partly. Yes."

"I thought so. What you said—the wording. It sounded like the Landfill Statutes. That's not my specialty. I haven't followed it closely but—wait—yes, of course—I forgot—there's a Medix facility down here. But—isn't it for fetal waste—Non-Natal Byproducts? We did a piece on all that—Governor Bebber's Landfill Program—this is way out of my field but it's for—for waste, isn't it? To reclaim swampland or something—rural reclamation?"

"They sometimes get away. The mistakes. I'm not sure how. But they do. At rest-stops. Bright lights attract them. I know that much. He must have seen your headlights from the woods—from his hiding-place. They all have hiding-places. They sometimes get away and find a place to hide. And then the lights come on—at night—it pulls them in. The highways are the worst. It's good he didn't come out fast enough tonight."

"You mean—look—this isn't how it's supposed to work—" he sat up in the chair, his hands a flutter-jab and clap together as he spoke. "I've at least read those laws—they've all been building on the federal directives for fifteen years or more—a drift toward neo-states' rights regarding abortion and public hygiene, health-care disposal—everything pretty much left up to the states. And even the new Bebber Landfill Law concerns only dead-matter—the byproducts of abortion, Last Resort Euthanasia, non-toxic waste—all left to the discretion of the individual counties to be used specifically for—"

"We're leaving tomorrow night. We would have left

sooner but my wife there was pregnant. So we waited for her baby. And then for her to feel stronger. She had a very hard delivery."

"Then—of course—I see—you're—"

"I know a way out—a logging trail. Back through the swamp. Almost to the Florida line. We're going there tomorrow night."

"And you've been taking them in—right? The—the run-aways? And those men in the woods—they're—"

"A part. Just a part. They do what they've always done. Did you damage your car?"

"What?"

"Your car—you said you left it. Is it wrecked?"

"No—no I saw I couldn't make it in the car. I left it where that creek cut through the road."

"You'll need to rest tonight. Tomorrow you can find your car. Those men out there will sleep till afternoon." Parker sat down on the floor beside the pallet, his eyes fixed on the green head there among the blankets and his voice turned soft, gone low and words droned out like spoken to himself alone. "They were out tonight, so they'll sleep. And you can find your car. We'll take you there—somebody will—through the woods. And you can go on down to Florida then. This baby will be fine. He's sleeping now. My nurse and I will clean him up. More rain tomorrow, I think. And fog. You'll need to wait till mid-morning to leave. I'll get you some dry clothes and take you to a place where you can rest. We don't have much food. We've packed most everything that's left. But there's enough still left out for some kind of breakfast surely. There'll be enough for that."

"But—but—" He stood up and shook his head,

beard still glistening and the firelight flickering out a shadow-dance across his arms and legs. “This is—obscene—it’s—it’s not supposed to be this way—”

The child squeaked once and clucked a few times more and Parker reached to pat it back to sleep again. Sparkles fanned out in the fireplace in a flattened sweep across the log and coals. A draft come down with raindrops there to hiss among the flames.

CHAPTER FIFTEEN

It was nearly dark. Four o'clock and black as deepest night outside. And rain sometimes a cold thing sounding on the window-glass and on the roof. The man was gone. He'd stayed a little while past breakfast, past what there was of FirstLight Singing with the sound like birds lost in the dark. He stood there in the room to talk some soft and low with Parker and a baby colored green. But Judy stayed in bed, the quilt and blankets warming all around and Baby Crystal Bea a coo and sometimes piglet grunt there close against her side. The man had tried to stay and help. But Parker sent him on his way as soon as it was light enough to see.

"I'll help you in Florida then. Publicity. It's not like this in Florida. I'll call some people I know. I can get you help. You just get there. Ok?"

"We'll get there."

"Good. Are you sure you don't want me here? I can drive. Load trucks. Something—"

"No. My man, Emment'll take you where you need to go. He knows the woods. You're not that far from where you left your car. And he'll help you all he can."

And they had talked some more but spoke too low to hear and she had dozed with Crystal Bea nudged to her breast, with tiny lips and mouth a pull and tug and piglet-sound there sometimes too a lazy thing around and close.

Then Parker standing near, a baby in his arms all green like spring-frogs in the tender grass and Crystal Bea a coo-grunt filled with milk and twisting with her hands and feet, a gentle rocking side to side that made a scraping sound upon the quilt. And Judy had smiled at Parker as he spoke, his face a floating thing like in a dream, the room beyond not clear at all but shadows there and creak of wood each time the wind got strong.

"I fixed the fire. It'll warm up things directly. Rest while you can. An' feed her good. We're leaving when the fog gets deep. I'll come back then. You rest now—till it's time to go."

She answered in a voice not even close to what she knew was really hers, had said some words that seemed too fat to make it through her teeth and up to where he floated on the growing dark. And Parker had patted her, had kissed her forehead and her lips, the Baby-Green there in his arms swung down to grin a second face against his own. The darkness had grown deeper all the day, the wind a howl sometimes and moan out on the porch and rain-sound strong above that made her wake up quick to see if anyone was there. And Baby Crystal Bea a pink and sucking piglet sometimes cooing like a mourning-dove, with perfect fingers, toes and ears and body smooth and bottom soft a snug and white against the diapers Big Nurse made. And doze and wake-up with a sucking sweet a pull and tug against her sending warm down to the places deep inside and clean now like the bottom-soft, the piglet-bottom when she made it white again and snug down in a diaper soft and deep. The day was ending when he came again.

"It's time. The trucks are about ready. Big Nurse will come get you. Feed the baby all you can. We won't make camp until we cross the state line."

And gone again before her fat words made it out.

But Big Nurse helping now, and warm begun to turn away, a cool and freshening feeling driving in instead and deep to bring her arms and legs to life, to help her move and quicker than she ever could down in the quilt-nest left behind.

CHAPTER SIXTEEN

Parker stood alone among the beds. The Bull-Rush Ward was quiet now, the nuns and Big Nurse gone and Doc and Emment busy with the grave. The smallest babies all had died and one by one it seemed, like some sad passing on of sleep, a naptime shared and moving swiftly from the first one touched down to the last. And there was nothing anyone could do to stop what settled in to stay.

The nightlights glowed against both walls and mobiles dangled up above the beds, slow-twisting even now a flash of clown-face, spotted horses, pigs and chickens there and something like an eagle on the wing. The beds stretched down from where he stood like boats at rest upon a water still and calm. His boots clicked loudly in the room, a slow walk in between each boat and one last look down at the sailors fast asleep, asleep and waiting for a tide and break of day, in dreams now whole and close and perfect like the dawn.

EPILOGUE

Night and Fog

The men were shoveling-in the clay, mud-slick and bubbled from the misting rain, the fog rolled in so thick the lanterns looked like tiny dots of light. A glowing ring around the pit. The clay made plop and sucking sounds down where they couldn't see.

"Somebody ought say something."

Emment's voice sounded tired, deep and raspy and with a cough come in to bump the words along. The other men were silent, shovels sucking up the clay, a push and shove sometimes and shake and scrape to clean the blades. The trucks and cars were idling toward the south, down past the place the Honor Barn had stood, their noses aimed at Sutter's Swamp and further in a winding twist and turn that ended near the Georgia line. And Florida a promise out beyond the night. No laws to hunt the babies there. No Medix dumping grounds and red smear on the sky.

"It ain't right just covering 'em like this. Somebody ought say something."

Emment rested on his shovel, handle close against his chest and slouch hat down across his eyes. The trucks were full, the Torsos and the rest, the rolling carts stacked neatly in the canvas bunks that Emment fixed. Two trucks and two old cars. The Hoppers and the Big Boys, Fun-Heads too would have to make it mostly on the ground. Just like the nurses and the nuns.

"Y'should of at least kept that reporter, Mr. Sledge. He'd of come in handy t'my way a thinkin'."

But Parker didn't seem to hear, his shovel pushing

in the last big mound of clay and then a pat before a jump down and a stomp across the top. A bird cried out from somewhere up above, behind them toward the wards and Recreation Hall. Back where the charges were all set and primed to blow an hour past the leaving time.

"Ain't y'going say something, Mr. Sledge?"

Parker stepped up from the covered pit, the mud thick-coated on his boots. The bird-sound now was close and moving toward the south, a piping there and quick, a singing lifting gladly on the dark and wet.

Other books by James Louis Fortuna Jr.

Available now from Lightnin' Bug Publishing:

Story Collections:

A Rock in a Broken Land: Scenes from the Progressive Apocalypse

The Gator and the Holy Ghost and Other Stories of a Slightly Reconstructed South

A Burning of Ducks and Other Stories

Novels:

Alas! The Poor Yoricks

A Rumor of Appomattox: Confessions of a Georgia Klansman

Hell Broke Loose in Georgia

Forthcoming:

From Sea to Shining Sea and Other Stories

About the Author

James L. Fortuna, Jr. lives in the Piedmont region of North Carolina. In 2015, he retired from teaching courses in English, Philosophy, Ethics, and The Holocaust. Currently, he is writing satirical fiction about a world swimming at and around him in ever increasing distortion and disorder. While writing as a Catholic traditionalist within this new world a-forming, he has concluded (and is happy to share) a few basic things that need to be kept in mind in hopes of maintaining steady footing into whatever future remains. First, his youngest grandson, Carter, ever-truthful, recently introduced the author as "the oldest man I know." The mirror each morning confirms his words and each day moves his perception closer to a final view. The author is grateful for the reminder. Secondly, it has become apparent to the author that the mention of "climate change" or "equity" or "BLM" or "CRT" (or any other combination of controversial letters) does not signal the beginning of a serious and substantial conversation. Sadly, this limits meaningful social interaction beyond "Good Morning" or "Hot/Cold one today, yes?" or "Nice looking dog you got there!" In brief, the author now finds himself without ambition beyond a growing aspiration to become minimally relevant. It should also be noted that he continues to be happily married to a woman vastly superior to him in all the ways that really matter. He continues to follow the Christian Way as best he can. And, finally, he hopes for permission to keep on writing until given permission to finally stop.

www.ingramcontent.com/pod-product-compliance
Lightning Source LLC
La Vergne TN
LVHW012103160826
845678LV00014B/2914

* 9 7 9 8 3 7 4 7 0 6 9 2 5 *